I0556096

# The Storm That Walks

## An Interactive Adventure Story #1

### J. G. Morcant

jminnovativemarketingllc

# Copyright

# Contents

# Chapter 1
## Introduction

## How to read this book

BEFORE THE STORM, THERE is always a silence.

This is a tale meant to be walked, not merely read. The words that follow are carved in the old way—meant to be chosen, weighed, and lived with. At many points in this book, you will be asked to decide what the Seer (you) does next: which path to take, which truth to speak, which relic to trust, or which voice to heed. Each decision will change the shape of the story, opening some roads while closing others. Some choices earn favor with the gods or spirits, while others leave marks on fate that cannot be erased.

When a choice is offered, follow the instructions at the end of the passage. Turn to the indicated chapter or scene and continue from there.

The story ending you reach is not chosen at the beginning, but forged step by step through judgment, courage, and sacrifice. There is no single true path. There is only the one you walk. You are the Seer. Your name, your face, your past—are yours to imagine. This story does not bind the Seer to shape or gender, only to sight: the ability to see what others cannot, and to endure what others would flee.

You are mortal, but you are marked. You were born under a sky split by lightning that did not strike, and since childhood, you have heard the land murmur when storms gather. You are not strong of body, but you are difficult to break. Truth clings to you, even when you wish it would not. You carry no crown, no army, and no certainty. What you carry instead is attention—of spirits, of gods, of things older than names.

Once your journey is complete, go back to the beginning and make different choices, to follow a new story with a new ending.

# Chapter 2
## The World at the Edge of Storm

As DAWN RISES OVER the Hill of Tara lately, the air feels wrong. Clouds hang low and heavy, bruised with thunder that rolls but never falls. The grass is wet with mist, though no rain has come. Ravens perch along the standing stones, silent, their black eyes fixed upon you as if waiting for a signal only they can hear.

The stones themselves, ancient markers of kingship and fate, are changing. Hairline cracks run through their rune-carved faces. A dull glow pulses beneath the surface, like lightning trapped in stone. When the wind shifts, you hear it. Not sound, but meaning. Broken words. Half-remembered truths. A prophecy shattered long ago, now straining to be whole.

You know this place. Every druid does. Tara is the heart of the land, the seat where rightful rule is tested, and false kings are unmade. Yet it has never felt like this. The land is not merely restless—it is afraid. From the fractures in the stones comes the first warning: A storm is coming, not of sky alone, but born of god and mortal truth divided.

The Godborn Storm—a being spoken of only in fragments—stirs when prophecy is broken, and balance fails. If awakened incomplete, it will scour Ériu into silence. If restored whole, it may cleanse the land or claim dominion over it. The stones do not say which. They never do. What they do say is this: "You are late. And you are needed."

The prophecy carved into the stones is no longer whole. Its fragments lie scattered across sacred sites, bound into relics, hidden within riddles, or guarded by beings who do not yield without cost. To restore it, you must travel through bog and fire, tomb and storm, bargaining with spirits, facing kings, and standing in judgment before the gods themselves.

Not every truth can be reclaimed. Not every relic can be carried. Some choices will strengthen the storm. Others will weaken it. Some will change what the prophecy becomes. The land will remember what you do here.

When you are ready, step forward. The first stone has already cracked, and its runes are waiting for your eyes alone. Turn the page. The storm is watching.

# Chapter 3
# The Cracking of the Stones

STANDING AMONG THE STONES on the Hill of Tara, mist creeps slowly across the hill in pale ribbons, catching on the grass and clinging to your boots. The world below is a dim wash of shadowed fields and sleeping roads, but here at the crown of the hill, the air tastes sharp, like flint struck against stone. No rain falls. Yet everything is wet, as though the land has been sweating beneath a weight it cannot name.

Above you, clouds press low—dark, bruised, coiling in slow spirals that seem to turn without advancing. Thunder mutters somewhere inside them, not the clean voice of a summer storm, but the dissatisfied growl of something that has been awake too long. The standing stones ring the crest of Tara like a broken crown.

You have known these stones all your life. Every druid does. You have walked this hill in frost and in heat, during rites of kingship and rites of mourning. You have traced the old carvings with careful fingers, learning where a spiral must never be closed, where a knot must never be cut too deeply. But you have never seen the stones like this.

Hairline cracks web across several of them, thin as veins, glowing faintly from within. The runes—spirals, wheels, knots-seem to shift when you look too long. Not moving as living things move, but turning, reweaving themselves, as though the stones are trying to remember something they were once forced to forget. Ravens perch atop the highest pillars, their feathers slick with mist. They do not caw. They do not quarrel. They watch you with a patience that feels deliberate.

You step forward. The grass yields beneath your boots, damp and resilient, but each step carries the weight of ceremony. You are not merely walking across a hill—you are being counted. Measured. The land is aware of you now. At the center of the ring stands the Lia Fáil, the Stone of Destiny. Weathered. Broad-shouldered. Carved with grooves so deep they resemble the lines of an ancient brow. Once, it cried out beneath the feet of a rightful king. Later, it fell silent.

Now, a crack runs down its face. It is thin, no wider than the edge of a blade, yet it glows with a dull silver light, as if moonlight has been trapped inside the stone and cannot escape—your breath stills. Even the mist around your mouth hesitates, hanging unnaturally in the air.

Then the crack widens. Not with the sound of breaking rock, but with the sound of a sentence being torn in half.  Cold spills outward. The mist recoils. The ravens lean forward as one. And suddenly you feel it—attention. Not sight, not sound, but the pressure of awareness, like deep water pressing against skin.

The Ancestral Chorus is near. You have heard them before, faintly, like voices beneath running water. Tonight, they are closer. Tonight, they are impatient. "Late," they whisper—not in your ears, but behind your eyes. "Always late, little Seer. The

stones waited longer than you have lived."
You swallow, tasting iron. You do not answer. Old laws hold fast: never speak first
to the dead.

Instead, you reach into your belt pouch
and remove a small bundle of cloth. Inside is a pinch of salt taken from your
own hearth—ordinary, humble, sacred.
You scatter it at the base of the Lia Fáil.
The mist stirs. The stone's glow brightens. Something beneath the runes shifts.
You lean closer, fingers hovering near the
crack. Cold radiates from it like winter
sealed in stone. Beneath the familiar carvings, you glimpse another pattern—finer,
deeper, deliberately hidden. A second in-
scription lay beneath the first. A prophecy.
Not forgotten. Buried.

"Who carved you?" you whisper before
you can stop yourself. The moment the
words leave your mouth, the sky tightens. Thunder rolls once, low and warning. Ozone sharpens the air. Around the
ring, other stones answer—cracks flaring
open like waking eyes. Three stones blaze
brighter than the rest. They stand equidis-

tant from the Lia Fáil, forming a deliberate triangle. Each bears a rune newly lit, as if written by fire:

A crowned spiral — KINGSHIP

A split wheel — STORM

A coiled knot like a vein or serpent — BLOOD

Your pulse hammers. The prophecy has not merely broken. It has offered itself. A raven hops down from its stone and lands in the grass before you. It tilts its head toward the crowned spiral, then the wheel, then the knot, then fixes you with a black, unblinking eye. "Begin," its silence says.

The Ancestral Chorus murmurs again. "Three doors. Three wounds. Choose what you believe broke the world. The hill will remember."

You stand at the triangle's center. Mist gathers close, sealing the space like a circle drawn for ritual. Beneath your boots, the earth feels alive—tense, expectant. You understand now. This is not about which truth you learn first. This is about which truth you trust. The Lia Fáil cracks wider. A rune-shard rises into the air—thin, sharp, humming with restrained fate. It waits for you. You close your fingers around it. Somewhere above the clouds, something ancient shifts—and notices you. The path forward is no longer singular. It never will be again.

Make your choice carefully, and continue reading on the page indicated.

"THE STONE OF KINGSHIP" on page 12, "THE STONE OF STORM" on page 14, or "THE STONE OF BLOOD" on page 15.
(Choose Carefully)

# Chapter 4
# The Stone of Kingship

YOU STEP TOWARD THE crowned spiral. The light within the crack turns pale gold. The stone's shadow stretches toward you like an outstretched arm. Voices rise—oaths spoken in halls, cheers that sound too loud, silence where truth should be. You place your hand on the stone. Cold floods you.

You see kings crowned without consent. Laws carved to protect power rather than land. The Lia Fáil stands silent while men pretend not to notice. A voice—not ancestral, but vast—speaks. "When rule is untrue, the land breaks first." The mark burns briefly into your palm. On the ground, you see a small fragment of stone. Picking it up, you recognize the rune markings. This is an Oath Stone fragment. This fragment reveals lies spoken by rulers. It weakens tyrants, but angers those in power.

Proceed on your path to The Broken Crown on page 16.

# Chapter 5
## The Stone of Storm

YOU STEP TOWARD THE split wheel. The crack burns white-blue. The air smells of rain that has not fallen. Your bones hum as if answering a distant call. You touch the stone.

You stand inside a storm that wears a shape. Lightning crowns it. Its voice fills your chest. "I am born when truth is turned into weapons." You see yourself holding shards of prophecy—guiding, commanding, failing. The rune scorches your wrist, cold and bright. At your feet lies a small rune shard. You pick it up and see that it is a small Storm-Sigil shard. This shard allows communion with storm entities. Each use increases danger. You think it could be useful, and slip it into your rune sack. Embrace your fate with The Living Storm on page 21.

# Chapter 6
# The Stone of Blood

YOU STEP TOWARD THE coiled knot. The glow deepens to ember-red. The air fills with memory-scents: smoke, iron, wool, birth. You touch the stone. You see a newborn lifted toward rafters as thunder listens. You feel lineage coil through you like a living thing. A whisper. "Blood is a door. A door opens both ways." The knot-mark settles into your flesh.

As you step toward the path, a thread drifts toward you on the breeze. You pluck it from the air. It appears to be old but strong. On closer examination, you recognize that this is an Ancestral Thread. This relic can reveal hidden blood ties, but using it costs vitality or memory. Everything has a price. Continue down your path to The Marked Lineage on page 27.

# Chapter 7
# The Broken Crown

YOU DESCEND FROM TARA with the crowned spiral burning faintly beneath your skin. It does not ache. It reminds.

Every step away from the hill feels like stepping deeper into a wound the land has learned to hide. The road winds downward through fields that should be orderly and tended, yet hedges lean drunkenly, boundary stones lie half-swallowed by grass, and scarecrows tilt as though exhausted by watching too long. People see you before you see them.

A farmer pauses mid-plow, gripping the handles as thunder mutters overhead. A woman drawing water from a well stops when the bucket rises black instead of clear. They do not ask your name. They know what you are. "A Seer," someone whispers. "Too late," another murmurs. A shepherd watches you pass with eyes too alert for the hour, fingers tight on a crook worn smooth by years of grip. "Storm coming," he mutters—not to you, but to the land. "Storm always comes when crowns sit crooked."

You walk on. By dusk, you reach the outskirts of Maelchon's seat, a timber-and-stone hall raised on old ground, its great beams rising from the earth like ribs, darkened by generations of smoke. Banners hang from the eaves, but their colors have faded unevenly, as though the dye itself has lost faith. The moment you cross the threshold, the Oath-Stone Fragment at your belt grows heavy.

Inside, the hall is loud, its great beams rising from the earth like ribs. Fires burn inside, bright and welcoming, but smoke escapes the roof in uneven plumes, as if the hearth itself cannot settle. Mead flows. Meat steams on platters. Voices rise in laughter that rings just a beat too long. You smell rot beneath the feast—subtle, but unmistakable. When a servant passes, a drop of wine splashes onto the floorboards and spreads black, seeping into the cracks. The Oath-Stone Fragment at your belt grows heavier.

King Maelchon sits upon his carved chair, crown set straight, jaw clenched in practiced ease. He looks every inch a ruler—broad-shouldered, richly clad—but his eyes betray him. They flick, counting exits, measuring threats. When he sees you, his grip tightens on his cup, and for a fraction of a heartbeat, fear slips through the mask. He recognizes you. A murmur ripples through the hall. Druids are welcomed here, controlled and contained, but a Seer marked by Tara's stones is another matter.

"Welcome," he says, voice smooth as polished horn. "You honor my hall. Tara sends its blessing, it seems. Sit. Eat. The storm will break before nightfall. We will speak after."

The crowned spiral in your palm pulses once. You know, with the cold certainty of prophecy, that this crown does not belong to him. Not because he stole it with blood, but because he wears it while knowing the land has rejected him. He rules by silence, not right. By habit, not truth. The land has not broken because Maelchon is weak. It has broken because he knows he is untrue, and rules anyway. The hall itself waits as you consider your response to the invitation and choose your path.

As the feast continues, you feel the hall respond to your presence. When Maelchon boasts, beams creak. When he laughs too loudly, a torch guttering nearby spits sparks like warning tongues. A choice presses in on you as surely as the storm pressing against the sky. If you speak now—before the people—you will tear the lie open. The land will answer. But violence will follow. Kings do not surrender crowns quietly. If you stay silent, you may learn more. Beneath this hall lie older stones—older than Maelchon, older than kingship itself—laws that bind the ruler to the land, not to the throne.

Thunder rolls again, closer. Maelchon raises his cup. "You look troubled, Seer. Have the stones spoken ill of me?" All eyes turn toward you. The hall waits for your response, holding its breath.

A. Knowing Maelchon is a false king, you expose the lie before the people? You stand where all can see you. You speak the truth of Tara aloud. The Oath-Stone Fragment burns, and the words cannot be softened. The crown on Maelchon's head cracks, and the hall shakes. Outside, thunder answers. The land reacts violently, and you move to the Feast of the Broken King, on page 38.

B. Knowing Maelchon is a false king, you seek the law beneath kingship. You bow. You accept bread. You play the quiet guest. That night, you slip from the hall to uncover what kings were meant to serve. Descending beneath the hall to the stones beneath, the older stones, older than kings, you begin searching for the law that existed before crowns. The land listens as you proceed to The Law Beneath Stone, on page 51.

# Chapter 8
# The Living Storm

YOU DO NOT WALK away from Tara. You move into weather. The path down the hill dissolves almost immediately, not into mist or shadow, but into pressure. The air thickens around you, as if the sky itself has lowered its weight. Each step forward feels less like crossing ground and more like pushing through an unseen current. Your cloak pulls oddly against your legs, not from wind, but from competing forces—eddies of air twisting without direction or sound.

Behind you, Tara does not vanish. It recedes, as though the hill is choosing to let you go rather than being left behind. The split-wheel mark on your wrist begins to hum—not painfully, but insistently, like a struck tuning fork held too close to the body. With every distant roll of thunder, the vibration deepens, echoing through your bones and settling behind your eyes.

Your breath fogs, though the air is not cold. It tastes sharp, metallic, alive.

Clouds shift as you move. Not following, not fleeing, but adjusting. Gaps close. Shadows rearrange themselves. At times, you have the unsettling sense that the sky is making room for you. The land changes subtly at first. Grass grows shorter, tougher, its blades edged with silver sheen as though brushed repeatedly by lightning. Trees thin and twist, their branches reaching upward at sharp, unnatural angles, as if frozen mid-gesture of surrender or defiance. Birds vanish. Insects go quiet. Even the earth beneath your boots feels altered—harder, faintly warm, humming with restrained force.

By the time night approaches, you realize something unsettling: You have not seen the sun set. Light simply diminishes, drawn upward into the clouds, leaving the world below cast in a dim, storm-colored twilight. The sky presses closer now, its layers visible—rolling masses within masses, movement folding in on itself. Your thoughts begin to fragment, not into fear, but into patterns.

You notice that thunder never repeats the same cadence. How the wind coils and uncoils like a breath being carefully measured. How lightning crawls inside the clouds rather than striking downward, sketching fleeting sigils that vanish before meaning can fully form. You understand, with a quiet jolt, that this is not merely a storm gathering. This is a realm forming.

By nightfall, the land rises into a high ridge scarred by lightning strikes. Stones here are split and glassed, their surfaces blackened and smoothed by centuries of storms breaking against them. Some are fused unnaturally, as though struck while molten. Others bear shallow carvings. Old, unfinished, half-erased by heat. This is old ground. Dangerous ground. A place where druids once climbed seeking communion and learned, too late, why most gods prefer silence.

The Storm-Sigil Shard vibrates violently now, tugging toward the ridge's crest as if drawn by a lodestone. When you hold it, the hum aligns with your pulse. For a moment, you cannot tell which rhythm is yours and which belongs to the sky. Wind howls without direction. Surging and collapsing in irregular waves that buffet you from all sides. Rain does not fall. It gathers, heavy and expectant, hanging within the clouds like breath held too long. Lightning crawls above, branching, recoiling, testing. Searching not for ground, but for permission. And beneath it all, beneath sound and sensation, you feel something else awakening.

Attention. The Storm has noticed you. You are no longer merely beneath the sky. You are within its reach. Then the storm speaks. Not with sound, but with pressure. With meaning. "Seer." The word lands inside your chest, heavy enough to steal breath. The clouds churn, drawing shape. A vast form emerges—limbs of wind, a crown of turning lightning, a face that flickers between man, god, and stone. "You touched my fracture." "You carry my unfinished name."

You brace yourself against the gale. "Why are you waking?" you shout. Lightning forks. The storm's response is almost amused. "I was never asleep." "I was divided." Images tear through your mind: standing stones shattered into glowing runes; those runes driven into the hearts of kings and priests; truth sharpened into weapons.

"Restore me," the storm intones, "and I will cleanse."

"Bind me," it continues, "and I will obey."

"Ignore me," it finishes softly, "and I will devour."

You realize, with a chill deeper than fear, that the storm is not attacking Ériu. It is assembling itself from broken prophecy. The wind presses you to one knee—not submission, but acknowledgment—power hums just beneath your skin, inviting, terrible, intoxicating. You could open yourself to it. Let it guide you. Become something more than mortal. Or you could attempt the forbidden rites. Old, dangerous sigils meant to cage divine forces—many who tried before you are remembered only as scorch marks. Thunder roars overhead. The storm waits.

A. You do not raise your hands in command. You lower them, loosen your breath, and allow the storm to press inward rather than be held at bay. The sky responds immediately—lightning drawing closer, wind settling into a measured rhythm that matches your pulse. Knowledge arrives not as words, but as sensation: pressure, timing, hunger, restraint. Somewhere inside you, something human bends—not breaking, but no longer resisting. Continue your journey with "The Storm's Whisper" on page 46.

B. You step onto the scorched stone and carve sigils where lightning has already bitten the earth, using the storm's own scars against it. Each mark burns as it forms, the air tightening with outrage as the clouds recoil, then surge. The wind howls sharper now, no longer curious but challenged, its attention fixed wholly upon you. This is no plea and no communion—it is a declaration that the sky itself must answer. Proceed to The Binding Rite on page 61.

# Chapter 9
# The Marked Lineage

THE COILED KNOT BENEATH your skin tightens with every step. You leave Tara behind, but memory walks closer. Smells sharpen—smoke, iron, wet wool. Faces half-remembered surface unbidden, their eyes knowing too much.

Your path leads into the high hills, where the living tread carefully. At its end stands a bone-hut, half-buried in earth, roofed with antler and hide, as though trying to crawl back into the ground. Smoke curls from a hole in the roof. Inside waits Cairenn of the Long Memory, hunched and ancient, eyes clouded yet piercing. Bones and carved lineage sticks hang from the rafters, clicking softly as you enter. "You are early," Cairenn rasps. "Or late. Blood never keeps time."

Cairenn of the Long Memory does not belong to the hills—only to what the hills refuse to forget. They are older than any living druid, older than some of the standing stones, though no one agrees how that can be so. Some say Cairenn was once mortal, bound by oath to remember what kings ordered erased. Others claim they are a vessel—each generation pouring memory into the same waiting flesh, until time itself lost track of where one life ended and the next began. What is known is this: Cairenn remembers bloodlines the land itself has tried to bury—names cut from history. Children hidden, claimed, sacrificed, or crowned. When truth becomes too dangerous to speak aloud, it is given to Cairenn instead, to be held until the world is strong enough to bear it again.

They set a bowl before you—dark liquid, bitter and metallic. "Drink," they say. "And remember." The Ancestral Thread tightens painfully around your wrist. You drink—the world fractures. You see births marked by thunder that never strikes. You see kings tracing lineage into gods, then hiding the truth beneath law and crown. You see your own bloodline twisted into prophecy like a net cast too wide. Pain wracks you as memory floods in—not all of it yours.

"You are not the only door," Cairenn murmurs. "But you are one of the few who know it is a door." The truth settles like a stone in your chest: The storm listens to your blood. Not because you summoned it—but because something ancient runs through you. Something unfinished. You could accept this. Claim what stirs in your veins. Power would answer—but you would never again be entirely mortal. Or you could sever the thread. Cut the lineage's hold. The cost would be memory, pain, and the cold withdrawal of ancestors—but the land might breathe easier for it.

Cairenn watches you closely. "Choose," they say. "Before the storm chooses for you."

A. You let the Ancestral Thread tighten instead of fighting it, allowing the old power to settle fully into your bones. The pain sharpens, then steadies, transforming into something vast and attentive—like a storm learning your name. Cairenn's eyes soften with something like sorrow as the lineage awakens, no longer dormant, no longer denied. You feel the boundary between mortal and divine thin, stretched by blood that remembers gods too well. Whatever you become next, you will never again be untouched by the sky. Proceed to "God-marked Flesh" on page 91 to continue your adventure.

B. You grasp the Ancestral Thread and pull—not gently, not ceremonially, but with deliberate finality. Pain flares white-hot as memory tears away, voices fading into a cold, ringing silence. Cairenn exhales slowly, as though witnessing a death they have seen too many times before. When the pain passes, the storm's attention dulls, no longer intimate, no longer personal. You remain mortal—but something ancient has turned its face from you, wounded and watching. Proceed to "The Quiet Vein" on page 97.

# Chapter 10
## The Storm Unmoored

YOU TWIST THE RITE while it is still alive. The sigils are half-formed, the storm half-caught—balanced on a knife's edge between submission and eruption. You feel the pressure building too fast, too violently, the binding unable to hold what it was never meant to fully contain. The sky strains against its own compression, lightning screaming soundlessly within the clouds. You do not stop the ritual. You redirect it.

Your hands blur as you carve a new channel into the scorched stone, cutting across the original sigil lines at sharp, deliberate angles. The motion tears a cry from your throat—not of pain, but of effort—as you force the rite to bend rather than break. The air shrieks in protest. Wind slams outward, flattening grass in widening rings.

The storm falters. Then it slides. Not into you. Not back into the sky. Elsewhere.

The sensation is immediate and wrong, like shifting a weight from one bone to another and hearing both crack. Pressure bleeds away from the ritual ground, draining through the new channel you have carved. Lightning snaps sideways, lancing across the horizon instead of striking down. Thunder rolls—not overhead, but distant, confused. The binding holds. Barely. But something beyond the circle screams.

You stagger back as the ritual completes itself with a shuddering finality. The sigils dim, their lines scorched black and inert. The storm above loosens, clouds unraveling into ragged tatters, rain falling at last—not violently, but unevenly, uncertain. You have succeeded. And you have failed. The storm has not been destroyed. It has not been contained. It has been displaced.

Druin reaches you moments later, his face pale beneath rain and ash. He grips your arm, steadying you as your legs threaten to give way. "Where did it go?" he demands. You open your mouth—and stop. Because you do not know. The land answers before you can. A deep tremor ripples through the ground, not centered here, but far away—so distant it feels almost imagined. The rain around you slows, then stops entirely. Above, the sky clears too quickly, an unnatural calm settling like a held breath. Birds do not return. The silence is wrong.

You leave the ritual ground at dawn, moving across a land that feels subtly misaligned. Fields are intact. Trees still stand. But the air behaves strangely, thick in some places, hollow in others. Winds shift direction without reason. Clouds gather where they should not, dissipate where they should linger. The storm is no longer whole. It has been unmoored.

Villages speak of strange weather almost immediately. Not devastation—yet—but patterns breaking. Sudden gales in low valleys. Rain falling upward in coastal cliffs. Thunder without clouds. Clouds without rain that linger for days, oppressive and watchful. People blame druids. They blame kings. Some whisper your name. Druin walks beside you in silence for a long time before finally speaking. "You saved us," he says carefully. "But you did not save the world." You nod. The storm-force you diverted had to go somewhere. The rite demanded balance. Energy cannot vanish—it must be absorbed, translated, anchored. And something—somewhere—has taken it.

As days pass, reports arrive with growing urgency. A forest in the north where storms coil endlessly above the canopy, lightning crawling through branches like veins of fire. A stretch of coastline where the sea surges and recedes in violent, rhythmic pulses, as though breathing too hard. A mountain range shrouded in constant cloud, thunder echoing through its passes even under clear skies elsewhere. The storm has fractured. Each fragment still powerful. Each fragment unstable. Each fragment hungry. Ériu has not been spared—it has been divided.

Druin urges caution, restraint, time to study what has been done. But the land does not wait for wisdom. The storm-fragments grow more assertive by the day, reshaping local weather, bending animal behavior, warping the rhythms of life around them. Worse still—people begin to adapt. Some settlements learn to live beneath constant rain, building differently, farming new crops. Others harness the strange winds, using them for travel, trade, even defense. Where lightning strikes often, shrines rise—half-prayer, half-warning.

The storm is no longer a singular threat. It is a resource. And resources invite control. You stand on a high ridge one evening, watching distant thunder roll across three separate horizons at once. Druin joins you, his expression grim. "You have given the world options," he says. "Too many."

You feel it then—the subtle pull in your bones, weaker than before but unmistakable. The storm still knows you. Still recognizes your hand in its fate. It does not press inward, but outward, tugging at your awareness like a tide seeking shape. You could intervene again. You could gather the fragments, reassert control, impose unity through force of will and law. Bind the storm not to yourself—but to structure, to rule, to permanence.

Or— You could walk away. Let the storm-fragments remain wild and local, shaping regions differently, forcing mortals to adapt without divine guidance or central control. Chaos would persist—but so would choice. Neither path is clean. Neither path is safe. Druin watches you closely. "If you act," he says, "you may become something the world obeys rather than understands. If you do not... this land will never be the same."

You close your eyes. You remember the first crack in the stone at Tara. The prophecy splitting into shards. The warning implicit in its breaking: that no single ending was ever meant to hold all outcomes. The storm has been unmoored. What remains is not whether it can be controlled—but who pays the price of trying. The wind shifts again, carrying distant thunder from three directions at once. You breathe in. You must choose.

A. You impose order upon the fragments. You step forward and begin gathering the storm-shards, shaping them into a unified structure of law and containment. The land will stabilize—but only by bending around your authority. Continue the adventure in Dominion of Fractured Skies on page 222.

B. You leave the storm unbound. You turn away, refusing to dictate how Ériu must adapt. The storm-fragments remain wild, local, and unpredictable. The world will change unevenly—but on its own terms. Continue your adventure with The Age of Many Skies on page 251.

# Chapter 11
# The Feast of the Broken King

THE HALL IS TOO warm. Not the honest warmth of hearthfire and gathered bodies, but the fever-warmth of a place trying to convince itself it is well. Smoke clings to the rafters in slow layers. The torches burn steadily, yet their light seems reluctant to touch certain corners, as though darkness has taken root there and refuses to be named.

King Maelchon presides over his feast like a man sitting atop a lid he fears will blow off. He laughs loudly, drinks often, calls for music—anything to keep the hall's pulse loud enough to drown the quieter things: the creak of timbers under strain, the faint sourness beneath roasted meat, the odd way servants avoid stepping on the same floorboard twice.

Your presence has shifted the whole room. You feel it in the way conversations stumble when you pass. You see it in the way eyes flick toward your hands—as if the people expect Tara's mark to glow through your skin. The Oath-Stone Fragment at your belt has grown heavy as a river rock. It pulls at your hip with each breath, and when Maelchon speaks, it warms faint-ly—responding not to his voice, but to the truth (or lack of it) under his words.

"Eat," Maelchon says again, too kindly. "A Seer should not stand hungry in my hall." A platter is offered—the meat glistens. The steam smells rich. Yet when you look close-ly, the fat around the edges has a faint gray tint, as if the animal died frightened. A dog under the table noses toward the platter, then whines and crawls away. A storm grumbles outside. The sound is dis-tant, but it rolls through the floorboards all the same, like something massive shifting in sleep.

You take bread, because refusal here would be another kind of statement, and sit where Maelchon can see you, but not too close to his chair. He wants you close. He wants the hall to see you as his guest.

He wants your presence turned into proof. On the far side of the hall, you spot a figure who does not laugh. A druid in dark wool, hood shadowing his face. He drinks nothing. His hands rest flat on the table as if feeling vibrations through the wood. When your gaze catches his, you feel a sharp awareness—like a thorn under the skin. A rival. Or worse: a witness.

Maelchon follows your glance, then smiles too quickly. "Ah," he says. "You've met Druin, my counselor. A loyal voice. A steady hand." Druin inclines his head a fraction. No greeting. No blessing. Only a cold, measured assessment.

The music rises again—harp strings plucked hard, as if to force cheer into the air. The feast continues. Stories of hunts. Stories of victories. Stories of the old gods, told with that nervous brightness people use when they fear the gods might actually be listening.

Then Maelchon stands. The hall quiets immediately, chairs scraping, breaths catching. The king lifts his cup. "To Ériu," he announces. "To land and law. To Tara, that ancient seat of rightful rule!" Your Oath-Stone Fragment heats sharply, like a coal pressed against cloth. Maelchon continues, voice thick with practiced reverence. "—and to the gods, who favor my reign with peace." Outside, thunder answers—a single low roll that seems to come from the hill itself.

Peace. You feel the lie like a bruise. A servant crossing behind Maelchon stumbles. Their tray tilts. Wine spills across the floor in a dark sheet—then shifts color, blackening as if the wood drinks it eagerly. The servant freezes, staring down in horror. A murmur spreads. Maelchon's smile tightens. "Clumsy!" He snaps, too sharp for a king at celebration. The servant bows low, trembling.

And then you see it—the moment the hall cannot hide: beneath the king's chair, the carved legs are split with fine cracks, the wood spiderwebbed as if something inside is trying to get out. You recall the words from Tara: When rule is untrue, the land breaks first. The land is breaking under him.

Druin's voice slides across the hall, quiet but cutting. "Seer," he says, "Tara has not called loudly in many lifetimes. Tell us. Has the Lia Fáil cried again?" Silence falls like a stone. Maelchon looks at you with a warning in his eyes: Choose carefully. The people stare, hungry for certainty. Even the torches seem to lean inward. You could speak the truth now—rip the mask away and let the hall see the rot. Or you could play the king's game, swallow the truth long enough to slip beneath the hall later and uncover the older law that binds kings to land and prove it without bloodshed.

But the longer you hesitate, the more the hall feels like a trap closing. A child somewhere begins to cry. The mother hushes them, but the sound lingers, thin and sharp. Druin leans forward slightly. "Or has the stone remained silent?" he presses. "Some say Tara breaks only for those who threaten the rightful order." Maelchon's gaze does not leave you. The lie is layered—thick enough that if you speak, it will not merely expose him. It will expose everyone who has accepted him. The hall itself. Your palm prickles. Your Fate Mark pulses.

Outside, lightning flashes. Not striking, not yet, but bright enough that the hall's shadows jump across the walls like startled animals. You stand slowly. The floorboards creak under your weight, and the sound feels like an omen. In the sudden hush, you can hear the most minor things: grease popping in the hearth; a bead of sweat falling from someone's temple; the faintest hairline crack spreading in the wood beneath Maelchon's chair. The Oath-Stone Fragment at your belt hums like a held note. And you realize with cold clarity: whatever you choose, the storm will remember it.

A. You rise before the feast can swallow another lie, your voice cutting through music and murmured loyalty like a blade drawn too late to be ignored. You name what Tara showed you—the silence of the Lia Fáil, the fracture beneath Maelchon's rule—and the hall shatters into shouting, disbelief, and sudden, terrible relief. Cups overturn, benches scrape back, and hands go to blades as truth spreads faster than any command to stop it. Outside, the ground answers: thunder rolls low and wrong, and a tremor runs through the hill as if the land itself has leaned forward to listen. Oaths spoken here are no longer contained by walls or crowns—they spill outward, demanding judgment. Before guards can decide whether to seize you or shield you, the feast has already become a reckoning. Move quickly to The Bog of Sighs on page 68.

B. You let the feast continue, swallowing the truth like a held breath, and lean close enough for Maelchon alone to hear you. Your words are quiet, precise, and devastating: you know what Tara revealed, and you are willing to remain silent, for a price. The king's relief is instant, followed by calculation, followed by a fear that mirrors your own, because he understands exactly what you are offering and what it costs. Beneath the hall, beneath stone and song, doors still exist that lead to older law—places where power sleeps uneasily and remembers its first masters. Maelchon agrees, not because he trusts you, but because he cannot afford not to. As the feast roars on above, you feel the first weight of complicity settle into your bones. Discover the consequences of your decision in The Price of Compromise on page 75.

# Chapter 12
# The Storm's Whisper

"SEER." THE WORD ARRIVES inside your chest, heavy as stone. Your knees buckle. You catch yourself on a jagged rock, fingers scraping black glass where lightning has fused earth into sharpness. The clouds compress. A form emerges—vast and humanoid, made from wind and pressure and the intelligence of thunder. A crown of turning lightning arcs above its head. Its face flickers between shapes: a man's, a god's, a standing stone's rune-carved surface. It lowers toward you, and you feel your thoughts tilt, pulled toward it like iron toward a lodestone.

"You touched my fracture." "You carry my unfinished name."

Your throat is raw from the wind. "Why are you here?" you force out. "Why now?" Lightning ripples—silent, bright.

"Because you are late," the storm an-swers, and the words sound disturbingly like the Ancestors. "Because they buried prophecy in stone and thought stone was a coffin." The air stinks of ozone. Your skin prickles as if each hair is listening. "I am born," the storm continues, "when truth is divided into weapons." In your mind, images tear through like ravens: stones cracking; rune-shards rising; those shards driven into hearts—kings, druids, lovers, traitors—truth used as blade rather than balm.

"Restore me," it intones, "and I may cleanse."

"Bind me," it adds, almost amused, "and I will obey."

"Ignore me," it finishes softly, "and I will devour."

The last line chills you more than the wind. Devour what? Crops? Halls? Bodies? No memory. Meaning. The woven story of the land itself. You clutch the Storm-Sigil Shard and pull it free. The moment it sees open air, it glows white-blue, answering the being above. The storm's face steadies briefly, as if focusing. It leans closer. A whisper, so intimate it feels like breath against your ear, though the wind is roaring: "Let me show you how to survive."

The ridge vanishes. For a heartbeat, you are standing in a future: Tara's stones scattered across a plain, half-buried like bones. A crown lies twisted in mud. The people walk with heads down, eyes empty, as though they have forgotten what hope looks like. Then the vision shifts. A different future: you stand atop Tara's hill holding rune shards cupped in your hands. The storm-being kneels behind you like a weapon waiting to be aimed. You speak one word, and lightning strikes exactly where you command. Power. Absolute, terrible, clean.

Then one more vision, quietest and yet worst: You kneel alone in a grove, hands empty, while the storm circles above like a hawk. It does not strike. It does not rage. It simply waits... until you finally lift your head and offer yourself, because there is nothing else left.

The vision snaps away. You are back on the ridge, shuddering. The wind feels colder now, as if it has learned your fear. The storm watches you, patient. You realize it is offering you something no god should: guidance. Partnership. A way to shape the coming catastrophe rather than be crushed beneath it. But you also realize the trap: storms do not guide without cost. If you accept, you will carry its voice inside you, and it will change what "you" means. If you reject it, you may become its enemy—and enemies of storms are remembered only as ruins.

Lightning crawls across the underside of the clouds, sketching the split-wheel rune again and again as if writing a demand. The Storm-Sigil Shard grows hot in your hand. The storm leans closer. "Choose!"

A. Accept the storm's guidance. You still your breath and allow the storm's pressure to pass the skin and settle deeper, loosening the boundary between thought and sky. Lightning does not strike—you feel it translate, its language unfolding in sensation rather than sound. The storm shows you how it moves, where it waits, and how it chooses when to break and when to hold. Strength follows, and clarity with it, but something steady and human begins to blur, as though your footing in the world has softened. The storm does not claim you as a servant. It names you as kin. Move forward as Stormbound, on page 83.

B. Reject the storm as a lie. You draw your will inward and turn your face from the sky, denying the intimacy it offers. The pressure lifts at once, replaced by a sharp, cutting stillness that leaves your ears ringing. Lightning snaps violently through the clouds, no longer exploratory but furious, and the storm's voice returns altered, stripped of patience, sharpened by insult. What had hovered close in curiosity now withdraws, gathering itself with predatory intent. You are no longer being studied. You step toward The Unbound Tempest on page 104.

# Chapter 13
# The Law Beneath Stone

YOU BOW WHEN THE hall demands it. You take the offered bread with both hands, as custom requires, and let the warmth of the feast brush your face like a blessing you do not deserve. You listen to Maelchon's laughter, measured and too loud at the wrong moments. You watch his courtiers mirror him—smiling when he smiles, falling silent when his gaze sharpens. You let your eyes drift to the high beams where smoke stains the wood black, and you note how the shadows cling most stubbornly above the throne. A crown does not need to fit to be worn. A lie does not need to be believed to be obeyed.

When the night deepens, the hall loosens. Voices dull. Cups empty. Warriors slump into sleep with hands still near their blades. Somewhere, a harp string is plucked once—accident or omen—and the sound fades like a thread snapping. You rise quietly. Cloak pulled close. Breath held. You slip behind the tapestry that hides the narrow door Maelchon never uses in daylight. The stones beneath the hall are older than timber, older than song. Older than kings. The hidden stair accepts you.

It smells of dry earth and cold stone, of secrets held so long they have become part of the rock itself. Your torchlight slides over carvings half-erased, not by time alone but by intent. Spirals that should run unbroken are crossed through. Knots are cut open, their ends left raw as wounds. A law, once whole, has been made to stutter.

Halfway down, you hear another set of footsteps. You freeze. The torch hisses softly. Your heart becomes loud enough to betray you. A shadow moves at the top of the stairs—narrow, controlled, patient. Druin.

He does not speak. He does not call for guards. He descends slowly until his face catches the edge of torchlight. His expression is not anger. It is worry sharpened into suspicion. "You should not be here," he says at last, voice low enough to keep the stone from overhearing. "And yet," you answer, equally soft, "this stair exists."

Druin's gaze flicks to the carvings, then back to you. He carries no weapon in his hands, but his posture has the steadiness of a man who has stopped more than one desperate act with a look alone. "This is old law," he murmurs. "Older than the oaths in that hall. Older than Maelchon's right to pretend he rules."

You hear it in his tone—he already knows what you seek. Perhaps he has known for years, circling the truth without stepping fully into it. "You watched me," you say. "I watched the hall," Druin replies. "I watched what Tara would not bless." Your Fate Marks warm faintly, as if the land itself leans closer at the mention of Tara. Druin notices. His jaw tightens. "Some truths," he says, "do not repair what they reveal. They only break what is still holding." You do not answer. You continue downward. After a long breath, he follows.

The stair opens into a chamber carved directly from bedrock and not built—revealed, as if the stone was shaped by hands that asked permission rather than taking it. The ceiling is low enough to reflect sound downward. The air is dry, ancient, preserved like a sealed jar. At the chamber's center stands a broken standing stone. Not toppled by accident and broken deliberately.

Its upper third has been sheared away, the fracture too clean to be time's work. Runes spiral across its surface, interrupted at precise points—meaning severed mid-sentence. Where the carving should flow, it stutters. Where it should bind, it loosens. It is a law cut open, so it cannot close again—your torchlight trembles.

You step closer and feel something like gravity shift. Not physical weight, but authority. The sense that if you speak here, your words will matter more than they should. That if you lie, the stone will remember it like a stain.

Druin stops at the chamber's edge. He does not cross the threshold. "This is where it was done," he says, almost to himself. "Where kings decided they would no longer be chosen."

The thought lands cold in your chest. You kneel beside the fractured stone. The runes feel familiar in the way old wounds feel familiar—recognized by the body before the mind understands. Pre-royal law. Not a king's law. Not a druid's law. The land's law.

You trace one broken line with your fingertip. The air prickles. Your hand tingles as if brushed by distant lightning. For a heartbeat, the chamber hums. And the stone answers. Not with a voice, but with a pressure that brings images—not visions of possibility like prophecy, but memories of what was.

You see a time before crowns, when leaders were named by endurance and service. When the Lia Fáil cried out beneath a foot, only when the land recognized the step. When oaths were not decorations but bindings that shaped weather, harvest, and bloodline alike. You see druids sealing disputes by placing hands on stone and letting the earth itself weigh truth. Then you see the moment the old law was broken.

A group of men in fine cloaks, carrying chisels. A druid among them with eyes averted. The stone's runes are cut mid-spiral, severed so the land cannot finish speaking. And when it tries to answer—when the Lia Fáil begins to wake—someone strikes the fracture again. Again. Again. Until the cry becomes a crack and the crack becomes silence. The images vanish.

You are kneeling in torchlight again, breath shaking. Druin has not moved. But his gaze is fixed on your hands like he fears what your touch may awaken. "What does it say?" he asks. You swallow. Your tongue feels heavy, as if truth has weight. "It says kings were never meant to choose themselves," you answer. "They were meant to be accepted—or refused—by the land."

Druin's eyes close briefly. A long exhale. "And if you restore it," he says, "Maelchon falls." "Not only Maelchon." The words taste like stone dust. "Every crown that stands without the land's blessing." Druin's silence sharpens. He steps forward at last, just a pace, as if drawn despite himself.

"That would end wars," he says, and you hear the hope in it, buried deep. "Or start one that never ends." You look down at the broken runes. Your torchlight makes the fractures look like wounds. "I can mend it," you say, and the certainty frightens you. The knowledge sits in your hands as if it has been waiting to be used. "Not perfectly. But enough for the land to speak again."

Druin's voice is rougher now. "And if the land speaks... men will listen?" "They will have to," you say, because you have felt what this chamber does to lies. "Or the land will stop pretending it needs them." The chamber hums again—subtle, patient, as if Ériu itself is listening to the argument like a judge waiting for the final statement.

You glance at Druin. He looks older in this light, not aged by years, but by responsibility. He is not Maelchon's creature. He is something else: a man who has kept the hall from falling apart by holding his breath for too long. "I followed you to stop you," Druin admits quietly. "Or to make sure you did not die alone in here." "You think I might," you say. He meets your gaze. "I think the law you wake will not care whether you survive it." The truth of that settles into you like cold water.

You could restore land-based rule. Re-carve the runes. Let Ériu decide again who deserves to stand. It would shatter the comfort of inherited power across the whole island, shaking every hall and clan that has benefited from silence. Kings would lose certainty overnight. Some would kneel. Some would kill. The land would answer regardless.

Or you could seal it away. Hide the truth again beneath stone and precedent. Maintain order, even false order, long enough to prevent immediate collapse. Perhaps you could use the knowledge as leverage—quiet control rather than open upheaval. The land would remain restrained, still forced into silence. But silence is also a weapon.

You feel the chamber's attention on you. You feel the storm far above, moving somewhere beyond the roof and sky, as if even it senses that this law could reshape the world it intends to be born into—your hand hovers over the broken runes. Druin does not touch you. He does not interfere. But you can feel him watching like a conscience given form. "Whatever you do," he says, voice low, "it will not end with this room." You nod slowly. "I know."

A. You choose to restore land-based rule. You kneel beside the broken stone and begin to re-carve the severed spirals, letting the old law flow back toward wholeness. The chamber vibrates as if the bedrock is taking its first full breath in centuries. Druin stiffens, eyes wide, as though hearing something vast awaken beneath the hall. Above, every crown will feel the shift—some as relief, others as terror. The land will speak again, and kings will no longer be able to pretend they are its voice. Continue your adventure in The Land Without Kings, page 119.

B. You choose to seal the law away. You press your palm to the fractured runes and complete the erasure, burying the old authority beneath silence once more.

The chamber's hum fades until the air feels smaller, contained, obedient. Druin's expression tightens—relief tangled with dread—because he understands the cost of what you have chosen to preserve. Above, Maelchon's reign continues, and the hall remains standing—for now. Order holds, but the truth you have buried becomes a tool, and tools always demand a hand willing to use them. Continue your journey in The Shattered Prophecy, page 236.

# Chapter 14
## The Binding Rite

YOU DO NOT KNEEL. You step forward. The ground beneath your feet is scorched glass and fractured stone, a place where lightning has struck often enough to leave memory burned into the earth. The air here smells of iron and old rain. Even before you begin, the storm knows where you stand—not because you have called it, but because you have chosen to challenge it.

Wind snaps hard around your body, no longer curious, no longer circling. It presses from all sides, testing balance, searching for weakness. The clouds above recoil slightly, then surge inward again, thickening into a tight, roiling mass. Thunder rolls once, sharp and offended. This is not communion ground. This is a battlefield written in sky.

You draw the blade you reserved for this purpose—short, practical, already nicked from earlier trials. You press it to the stone and begin to carve. The first sigil burns as it forms. Not metaphorically. Heat flashes up your arm, searing nerves, forcing breath from your lungs. You grit your teeth and finish the line anyway, carving along a crack where lightning once split the rock. The symbol anchors itself there, faintly luminous, trembling like a trapped pulse.

The storm reacts immediately. Wind screams, rising to a pitch that rattles bone. Lightning forks low, striking the ground just beyond the sigil's edge. The air tightens, pressure building so fast your ears ring. Good. That means it feels the hook.

You carve the second sigil with shaking hands, sweat stinging your eyes. This one curves inward, a binding mark older than druidic circles—borrowed from half-remembered rites used once to cage river-floods and mountain-fires. You never believed they would work on something alive. The stone answers anyway.

The sigils do not glow evenly. They strain, edges flickering as if resisting their own purpose. The moment the third mark is cut, the sky convulses. Lightning slams into the ritual circle, stopping just short of your feet, crawling across the stone like a living thing. The thunder that follows is not distant—it is inside your skull, rattling thought loose from memory. The storm speaks. Not in words. In force.

Pressure crushes inward, testing ribs, spine, breath. Images tear across your mind unbidden: wind scouring mountains into bone, seas climbing cliffs, cities reduced to silence beneath endless rain. You feel its refusal—not as anger, but as the certainty of something that has never been bound and does not understand why it should be. You push back.

You carve the fourth sigil. This one costs blood. Your hand slips as lightning flares too close. The blade bites deep into your palm. Pain blooms hot and immediate. Blood spills onto the stone—and the sigil drinks it eagerly, flaring bright, anchoring the binding with something the storm cannot ignore. The clouds above contract sharply. The storm compresses. Not trapped—contained.

The wind drops suddenly, collapsing into a suffocating stillness. Lightning freezes mid-crawl, etched into the sky like a scar that refuses to heal. The thunder cuts off as if someone has clenched a fist around the sound itself. Your knees buckle. You drop to one knee inside the circle, gasping, heart hammering against ribs that feel too small to hold it. The sigils hum violently now, vibrating through stone and bone alike. You feel the storm pressing against the containment from every direction, probing, calculating. It is not defeated. It is learning.

Knowledge bleeds into you despite your resistance—not the fluid understanding of communion, but sharp, jagged insights torn loose by proximity. You feel the storm's structure: currents folded into currents, endless motion restrained only by balance and release. You understand, suddenly and horribly, what you have done. You have not ended the storm. You have compressed it. The pressure has nowhere to go.

Cracks spider outward from the ritual circle, racing across the stone. The sigils flicker, some holding, others warping under strain. The air begins to distort, sound bending strangely, as though the world itself is bracing. Your vision tunnels. You taste copper. And beneath it all, a deeper realization settles with sickening clarity: this binding cannot remain as it is.

Something must give. Either you tighten the containment—reinforcing the sigils, forcing the storm into an even smaller, more violent prison—or you redirect the pressure, altering the rite so the excess power escapes elsewhere. Neither option is safe. Neither is clean.

The storm presses again, harder this time, not in fury but in methodical insistence. It does not plead. It does not bargain. It simply applies force, the way gravity does, confident that eventually something will fail. You feel the prophecy unravel around this act. Not shattering into guidance or warning—but fraying, its strands slipping out of alignment. Futures that once branched cleanly now tangle. Outcomes blur. The storm is no longer moving toward destiny. It is reacting to confinement.

You stagger upright, teeth clenched, blood slick on your palm. The sigils pulse erratically now, some blazing, others dimming as the stone beneath them begins to fracture. The air smells of ozone and scorched earth. Time is no longer generous. You can feel it in your bones: if you hesitate too long, the binding will collapse on its own—and when it does, it will not be contained by intention or choice.

You must decide how this ends. Do you force the storm into submission, no matter the cost, tightening the prison until it breaks something fundamental? Or do you divert the excess—bleed the storm's pressure into the world itself, sparing yourself and this place, but scattering the consequences far beyond your sight? The sky above trembles. The stone beneath your feet groans. The storm waits—not patiently, but inevitably.

A. You tighten the binding. You reinforce the sigils, carving deeper, feeding them pain, blood, and will until the containment locks into place. The storm is forced into a narrower, more violent shape, its pressure screaming silently against its prison. The land around you begins to crack as the power compresses inward, seeking release that does not exist. Control is achieved—but at the edge of catastrophic failure. Continue in The Fractured Dominion, page 111.

B. You redirect the binding. You twist the rite at the last moment, carving channels to bleed the storm's excess force away from the circle and into the wider world. The containment holds, but only barely, and the pressure escapes in unpredictable surges that ripple outward across Ériu. You remain standing—but you have unmoored something vast, and it will leave scars wherever it settles. Continue to the next chapter, The Storm Unmoored, page 31.

# Chapter 15
## The Bog of Sighs

YOU DO NOT REACH the Bog of Sighs by accident. From the moment you turn away from blood's call and choose judgment over transformation, the land begins to lean downward, as if guiding you toward something it has long prepared. Roads soften beneath your feet. Villages thin. People you pass speak less, watching you with an unease they cannot name. Doors close earlier at dusk. Fires burn lower. Even the cattle grow restless beneath skies that feel heavier than they should. They know where you are going.

No one names the bog aloud. They never do. But when you ask for the low road east, faces tighten, and directions are given with hurried gestures rather than words. An old woman presses a charm of woven rushes into your hand without explanation. A child stares too long at your shadow, then is pulled away sharply by a parent who will not meet your eyes.

Stories follow you into the lowlands. Some say the bog listens. Some say it remembers better than stone. Some claim those who enter return altered. Voices quieter, eyes too knowing, or else not at all. Others insist these are lies told to keep children obedient and travelers on the road. Yet even those who laugh at the stories do not cross the bog after sunset.

By the time the land sinks fully, doubt has thinned to silence. Grass grows sparse and brittle. Soil darkens beneath your boots, drinking sound. The air thickens with the scent of rot and old water, sweet and sour at once. Each step pulls slightly, not enough to trap you, but enough to remind you that the ground here does not like to let go of what it is given.

The Bog of Sighs stretches before you. Black water lies broken by islands of reeds and skeletal trees, their branches reaching upward like fingers that once begged. Mist coils low, clinging to the surface as though the bog itself is holding its breath. The sky above is dim though the sun has not yet set, light paling and thinning as if reluctant to linger over a place that does not forget.

You feel it the moment you step closer. This place remembers promises—every oath sworn in desperation. Every vow broken quietly. Every truth swallowed for safety or power. They have weight here. They have gravity. Words spoken elsewhere sink faster than bodies ever could.

As you step onto the first patch of firmer ground, the water ripples outward, though you have not touched it. Circles widen, intersect, dissolve. Beneath the surface, shapes shift—suggestions of hands, faces, mouths opening in soundless exhale. You hear it then: not a voice in the air, but a presence pressing against thought.

"Who comes bearing unfinished words?" The mist parts slowly, deliberately. From the bog's heart rises the Bog-Warden. It stands taller than any person, draped in weeds, drowned reeds, and hanging moss that drips steadily back into the black water. Its form is half-human, half-root, as though something once mortal allowed itself to be claimed by the bog rather than die elsewhere. Water pours from its limbs as if it is always in the act of emerging and sinking at once. Where its eyes should be are two deep hollows filled with reflected sky—clouds moving where sight should be.

You feel your Fate Marks burn. "Seer," the Warden intones, its voice layered with many echoes, as though each word is spoken by more than one throat. "You walk with lies clinging to you like burrs. Some are yours. Some are not. All must be weighed." The water around your ankles grows colder.

You remember the king's hall. The storm's whisper curls too close to comfort. The ancestral thread is tightening and loosening beneath your skin. Every moment you chose not to speak. Every truth you spoke too loudly. Every silence that preserved you and every silence that sharpened the storm. Some truths. Some half-truths. Some truths left deliberately unspoken.

The Bog-Warden raises one dripping hand, and the mist tightens around you like a held breath. "Confess." The word strikes with the weight of a stone dropped into deep water. You understand then—this is no symbolic trial. No ritual gesture. The bog does not deal in metaphor. It deals in balance. It will take something. A lie. An oath. A future choice. A name spoken aloud that can never be taken back. And if the offering is insufficient, if the truth is too light, too carefully trimmed. It will take you.

You have heard the rumors—travelers who emerged from the bog quieter than before. Kings who returned altered, ruling more carefully or more cruelly than memory allowed. Wanderers who left something behind and could never say what it was. Children's tales insist the bog steals souls. Druids argue it steals only what should never have been carried so long. Looking at the Warden now, you suspect both stories are true.

You open your mouth—and hesitate. Do you confess the truth you have avoided, knowing it will bind you, expose you, and cleanse the land at a cost you cannot yet measure? Or do you attempt to hold something back, offering a partial truth heavy enough to satisfy the bog and light enough to survive? The water rises another inch. The Warden's voice deepens, roots creaking beneath the sound. "Choose what sinks."

A. You draw a breath heavy with the weight of everything you have carried and speak the truth you have most careful- ly avoided. The words sink into the bog like stones, pulling memories, oaths, and buried guilt down with them. The water trembles, then settles, as if relieved to re- ceive what it has long awaited, finally. The Bog-Warden inclines its head, not in ap- proval, but in acknowledgment of balance restored. Pain follows, sharp and cleans- ing, and then stillness—an absence where something dangerous once pressed. When you step back onto firmer ground, the land itself seems to exhale. Continue on The Path Of Reckoning on page 127.

B. You choose your words carefully, shaping a confession heavy enough to satisfy the bog without revealing everything it demands. The water grows quiet, unnaturally so, and the mist coils tighter around your legs as if listening for what you did not say. The Bog-Warden does not challenge you; instead, it watches as something unseen settles its weight against your shadow. The offering is accepted—but incompletely—and the bog records the debt in silence rather than sound. As you turn away, the air behind you feels thicker, damp with breath that does not belong to you. You leave the bog alone, but not unaccompanied. Moving on with The Lingering Curse on page 134.

# Chapter 16
# The Price of Compromise

MAELCHON'S HALL DOES NOT truly sleep. It quiets, yes—the music fades, the last cups are cleared, the torches gutter lower—but beneath the timbered roof, tension lingers like smoke trapped between beams. Even as servants withdraw and guards settle into uneasy watch, the stone remembers what has been spoken here. It remembers what has been withheld. You feel that memory press against you as you stand at the edge of the dais, the king's laughter still echoing faintly in your ears. The bargain has been struck. Silence, carefully measured and deliberately offered, in exchange for descent.

Maelchon does not thank you. He simply rises, adjusts his cloak, and steps toward a narrow door half-hidden behind a tapestry depicting Tara as it once was—whole, crowned by sky and stone alike. With a

practiced hand, he presses a carved sigil you would not have noticed had you
not been watching so closely. Stone grinds
against stone. A seam opens. The stairs
beyond breathe cold.

You follow, every instinct protesting, even
as your mind catalogues details with brutal clarity. This is how compromise begins—not with a blade, but with a door that
should not exist. The stair spirals downward, narrow and uneven, cut directly into
bedrock. Your torchlight struggles here,
shadows folding back on themselves, making the descent feel longer than it should
be. The air grows dry and sharp, carrying none of the damp rot of the bog nor
the charged tang of storm. This air is preserved. Contained. Older than the hall.
Older than Maelchon. Older than any king
who has sat above it.

The walls bear carvings—half-erased, deliberately defaced. Laws etched before
crowns. Before thrones. Before any ruler
dared claim Tara's authority as an inheritance rather than a trust—spirals bound
by chains. Knots cut open, their ends left

raw and unresolved. You recognize the violence in the work. This was no erosion of time. This was erasure. Your Oath-Stone Fragment warms against your chest, responding to the carvings with a low, uneasy pulse.

Maelchon descends only partway. When the stair narrows, he stops, his face half-lit by torchlight, the rest swallowed by shadow. "You will find what you seek," he says quietly. "And when you do, you will understand why some truths cannot be spoken aloud." The calm in his voice unsettles you more than anger would have.

Behind him, another presence shifts. Druin. You had not heard him follow, but you feel his attention now—sharp, measuring, wrapped in stillness. He does not speak. He does not descend. He simply watches from the threshold, eyes reflecting torchlight like a blade held just out of sight. Whether he is here to witness, to warn, or to remember, you cannot tell.

Maelchon turns away. The stone door grinds shut above, sealing you below. The stair opens into a circular chamber carved directly from the bedrock of Tara—the Law Chamber. Your breath catches, not from awe, but from recognition. This place hums with dormant authority, the kind that does not need voices to assert itself. The walls curve inward slightly, not oppressive, but deliberate, as if shaped to focus attention toward the center.

There stands the stone. Once a standing stone like those above—upright, honored, answered by the land, it now lies toppled and broken, its upper third sheared away. Runes spiral across its surface, fractured with surgical precision. Where lines once flowed, they have been interrupted, redirected, scarred. You kneel without realizing you've done so. This was not decay. This was strategy. The old law—the land choosing ruler, the stone crying out beneath rightful feet—was not lost. It was dismantled.

Kings did not wait for the land's voice. They silenced it. They broke the law into fragments small enough to bury, hide, and forget. What remained above became ceremony. What mattered was sealed below.

Your torch flickers violently. For a moment, you swear the chamber darkens. Not from lack of light, but from pressure. As if the stone itself is leaning closer, waiting. You touch the broken runes.

The chamber responds—a low vibration rolls through the floor, subtle but unmistakable. Your Fate Marks flare painfully. The Oath-Stone Fragment burns hot, nearly slipping from your grasp. Images flood you—not visions, but consequences.

You see kings stumbling as authority drains from them overnight. Crowns growing heavy, meaningless. You see the land reasserting itself—harsh, unyielding, fair in ways people have forgotten how to endure. You see villages choosing leaders rather than inheriting them. You see chaos and then adaptation.

You also see the alternative. Order preserved. Stability maintained. Kings ruling carefully, aware of the buried truth beneath their feet. Corruption deepens quietly, layered beneath law and precedent. The land groaning, but holding. Both paths are absolute. Both are dangerous.

A sound echoes faintly from the stairs. Footsteps. Slow. Deliberate. Maelchon waits above, yes. But Druin watches. You feel his presence like a held breath. He has not interfered. Not yet. Perhaps he is not here to stop you. Perhaps he is here to remember which choice you make.

You rise slowly, torch held high. You could restore what was broken. Re-carve the runes—Rebind kingship to land. Let Ériu decide who stands and who falls. The cost would be immediate and brutal—but honest. Power would shift beyond anyone's control, including yours. Or you could seal the law away again. Hide it deeper. Layer truth beneath silence once more. Preserve order. False order, perhaps, but order nonetheless. Collapse delayed. Bloodshed avoided. For now. Your hand hovers over the fractured stone. Above you, the stairs creak softly. Time is running thinner.

A.  You do not restore the broken runes as they once were, nor do you erase them completely. Instead, you alter them—subtly, deliberately—allowing the land's authority to breathe again while hiding its voice beneath layers of ambiguity and restraint. The stone answers, not with a cry, but with a tightening silence, as though something ancient has agreed to wait. Kings will keep their crowns, believing themselves secure, even as unseen limits close around their rule. Power will fracture quietly when abused, failing without warning, leaving no apparent cause to name or resist. When you rise, the chamber feels unchanged—and that is the danger. You leave knowing Ériu will be governed not by truth or lie, but by consequences no one will ever fully understand. Continue your story in The Veiled Law on page 244.

B. You hesitate only long enough to understand what you are preserving, then complete the erasure with steady, deliberate care. The broken stone willingly absorbs the silence, its hum fading until the chamber feels smaller, contained, obedient. The land's pressure recedes—not relieved, but restrained—and a fragile stability settles into place like a lid sealed too tightly. Above, Maelchon's crown remains secure, its fractures hidden from those who need not know. Order survives, at the cost of truth, and the debt you have buried will not remain quiet forever. You turn away knowing you have bought time, not absolution. Take The Controlled Ending Path on page 258.

# Chapter 17
## Stormbound

THE STORM NO LONGER waits above you. It moves with you. Wind curls inward when you breathe, drawn toward your lungs as if seeking instruction. Thunder no longer follows lightning—it answers your heartbeat directly, rolling through the sky in the same uneven cadence that pulses behind your ribs. The Storm-Sigil Shard has ceased to exist as a thing you carry. It has become a tension threaded through your bones, a constant awareness of pressure and release, like a joint you never knew how to move until it began to ache.

You feel heavier and lighter at once. When you walk, the air resists you, then yields. When you pause, clouds tighten overhead, as though your stillness disrupts a balance the sky is struggling to maintain. The line between motion and consequence has thinned. You sense that if you linger too long in any one place, the storm will finish gathering whether you will it or not.

Others sense it too. People look up before they see you. Conversations falter. Dogs whine and pull away from your path, hackles raised. Horses shy sideways, nostrils flaring, refusing to cross your shadow. Hearth fires gutter low as you pass, flames bending away as though deprived of breath. Even bells sound wrong near you, their tones flattened, stretched thin by pressure in the air. You learn quickly not to remain among them.

The land ahead opens into a broad, high plain where grass grows short and pale, pressed down by centuries of wind. This place once held sacred circles—stones raised to speak with sky and earth alike—, but they now lie scattered like broken teeth, toppled and half-buried. Some bear scorch marks. Others are split cleanly in two, fused at the edges as if lightning once struck while they were molten.

Here, the storm slows. Clouds spiral inward, lowering until the sky feels close enough to touch. The light dims, not into darkness, but into a strange, metallic twilight that flattens distance and depth. The air hums. Static prickles along your skin. Hair lifts at your nape and arms, standing on end as though responding to a call only it can hear.

Lightning does not strike. It crawls. Thin filaments branch along the ground at your feet, tracing slow, deliberate paths through scorched grass and cracked soil. Each line hums softly, alive and attentive, never quite touching you, never straying far. The storm has drawn a boundary—and placed you at its center. "You listen," it says. The voice does not come from above or around you. It forms where sensation becomes meaning, where pressure resolves into understanding. There is no threat in it. No promise. Only recognition. "You adapt." The words settle into you like a weight finding its balance.

The storm presses closer, and the pressure increases until your joints ache and your breath comes shallow. It does not crush you. It tests you—measuring how much force you can bear before you yield or shatter. You sink to one knee, palms pressed to the ground, feeling lightning vibrate beneath the soil like a second pulse—knowledge floods in, not as visions or prophecy, but as instinct. You understand how storms choose their paths—how they follow fractures in air and intention alike. You learn where pressure gathers, where it hesitates, where silence can redirect force more effectively than resistance. You grasp how thunder is not merely sound, but timing; how lightning is not chaos, but decision.

You realize with a jolt that the storm is not teaching you domination. It is teaching you grammar. Your thoughts begin to blur at the edges, stretched thin by the sheer scale of what you are absorbing. The sense of where your body ends and the sky begins wavers. For a heartbeat or two, you are certain that if you let go entirely, you would no longer need to stand. Gravity feels optional here, something negotiated rather than obeyed.

As understanding deepens, another truth surfaces—quiet, unsettling in its simplicity. Storms do not gather only around will. They gather around places. You feel it now in the land beneath your palms: fault-lines where pressure pools, ancient plains where air thickens more readily, ridges that draw lightning as surely as blood once did. Flesh was never the storm's only doorway—only the most immediate one. The circles that once stood here failed not because they were weak, but because they tried to bind intention instead of boundary. The storm needs an edge it cannot cross. A horizon it must obey.

The storm's presence deepens. "You could guide me," it says, and now there is something like curiosity in the pressure of its attention. "Shape where I fall. Decide what breaks." The possibilities unfurl before you—not as visions, but as futures implied by understanding.

Storms turned aside from villages at the last moment. Floods are delayed until rivers can bear them. Lightning striking only where it must—fire-clearing, boundary-marking, never wanton. The land would fear you, yes, but it would endure. You would become the storm's interpreter, its boundary, the living threshold between sky and stone. And in doing so, you would lose something vital. You feel it clearly now: the steady grounding of mortality. The small, necessary limits that keep a person anchored in flesh and time. To accept the storm entirely would mean letting those limits erode, replaced by something vast and patient and utterly indifferent to human scale. You would not vanish—but you would no longer belong entirely to the world you once walked.

Another possibility rises alongside it, dangerous, reckless, undeniable. You could turn the storm inward. You understand how it might be done—where the gathered pressure overlaps, where tension strains against itself, where a single, catastrophic redirection could force the godborn storm to collapse into its own weight. You see the fault-lines clearly now, etched in air and force. The cost is unmistakable. This would not merely wound you. It would unmake you.

Your body protests at the thought, instincts screaming survival even as understanding insists the option exists. Lightning flares brighter, the crawling lines tightening their circle as if sensing the decision before it is spoken. Pain blooms preemptively along your spine, a warning written directly into nerve and bone.

The storm does not urge you. It waits. The wind stills completely. The hum deepens, steady and expectant. For a long moment, the world holds its breath, balanced on the edge of what you will choose to become.

A. You loosen the last grip of resistance and allow the storm's cadence to settle fully into your breath and bone. The pressure eases—not because the storm withdraws, but because you have learned how to hold its weight. Power unfolds with terrible precision, reshaping thought and instinct until the sky's grammar feels as natural as your own heartbeat once did. You feel the slow thinning of what made you singular, human, replaceable. In its place rises something vast enough to be trusted with devastation. When the storm acknowledges you, it does so without reverence, only recognition. Continue to The Ascension of the Stormwarden on page 152.

B. You refuse to carry the storm within yourself. You understand now that the storm does not require you. It requires a boundary—something wide enough to hold its force, firm enough to deny it passage beyond a chosen edge. Flesh was only ever the nearest vessel. You rise, not in defiance, but in refusal, and turn your will outward—toward land, toward horizon, toward a place that will bear the weight you will not. The pressure shifts immediately, drawn away from your bones and into the wide skin of the world. The storm resists, then settles, finding its limits written not in blood, but in stone and distance. You will walk free—but the land will never forget where the sky was taught to stop. Proceed to The Bound Horizon on page 281.

# Chapter 18
## Godmarked Flesh

YOUR BLOOD NO LONGER feels contained. It hums beneath your skin, a low, resonant vibration that answers thunder before sound reaches you. Each pulse carries intention. Each breath stirs something vast and attentive. The Ancestral Thread burns bright now, no longer subtle, no longer patient—its presence unmistakable, etched into muscle and marrow alike. You feel watched, not by eyes, not by spirits skulking at the edge of perception, but by forces that measure worth in endurance rather than intention. The air itself seems to lean toward you, charged and expectant. When you lift your hand, the wind adjusts. When your heart stutters, lightning flickers somewhere far above.

You stand alone on a high rise overlooking Ériu. The land spreads below you in shadowed layers—fields, rivers, darkened villages clinging to warmth and routine. Smoke rises thinly from hearths. Lives continue, unaware that the sky has begun to turn its attention elsewhere. Clouds spiral inward overhead—not toward Tara, not toward any sacred stone, but toward you.

The realization settles with terrifying clarity: You are no longer standing beneath the storm. You are becoming its axis. The godborn storm does not rage. It gathers. Its patience is vast, ancient, and precise. It is waiting to be born through something worthy. Through flesh that remembers thunder not as destruction, but as lineage. Through you.

Your bones ache with the strain of it. Not pain exactly—more like expansion, as if your body is learning how small it once was. Memory comes unbidden now, not as vision but as inheritance. You feel other lives brush against your own: ancestors who carried fragments of this same fire, who bent beneath its weight or were broken by it. You feel where they faltered, where they were crowned, where they vanished into story.

The Ancestral Chorus gathers close. They are no longer whispers beneath thought. They sing. Their voices braid together—joy and grief indistinguishable—as they recount names long erased, deeds remembered only by stone and blood. They do not urge you forward. They do not warn you away. They sing because this moment has been waiting longer than any of them have endured.

You understand the choice before you with brutal clarity. If you accept what your blood offers—if you step fully into what is awakening—then the storm will answer you completely. You will gain the authority to seal other blood-doors forever—no more godborn catastrophes. No more lineage twisted into weapons. The sky will kneel when you command it. But you will not remain as you are. Mortality will thin. Memory will blur at the edges. Relationships will soften, then loosen, until they become stories rather than bonds. You will walk among people as something already becoming legend, already slipping out of time. They will fear you, revere you, curse you, pray to you—and none of it will feel quite real. You will become myth while still breathing.

The other path is darker in its own way. You could end the line entirely. You feel how it might be done—where the Ancestral Thread could be grasped and burned away, not severed cleanly, but destroyed. The divine blood would be unmade, its power collapsing inward until nothing remained that could answer the storm's call. The godborn tempest would lose its favored path, forced to dissipate or fracture without an anchor strong enough to sustain it. The cost would be severe.

The power has threaded itself too deeply now to be removed without consequence. You would lose more than magic. More than lineage. Parts of your self—memory, identity, perhaps even the sense of where you end—would be torn away in the severing. You do not know what would remain afterward. You only know the land would be safer for it. The storm tightens above, lightning sketching vast, slow arcs within the clouds. It does not threaten. It waits.

Your body trembles—not from fear, but from the strain of holding so much possibility at once. The air hums louder now, pressure mounting, as if the sky itself is leaning closer to hear your answer. You think of the villages below. Of children taught stories to keep them obedient. Of kings who bent law to suit inheritance. Of ancestors who carried this burden in fragments, never knowing whether it would redeem or destroy. The Chorus swells, voices rising into something like harmony and lament combined. Whatever you choose, there will be no return to what you were. You lift your gaze to the storm.

A. You open yourself fully to what your blood has always promised, allowing the Ancestral Thread to blaze without restraint. The storm answers immediately, its vast pressure folding inward until it kneels, recognizing you as the threshold it has awaited. Apotheosis is not gentle, but it is complete, reshaping you into something capable of holding the sky's weight. You rise changed, no longer bound by mortal limits, and the land feels your presence as both protection and warning. Continue with The Last Blood Door on page 207.

B. You seize the burning Ancestral Thread and turn its power against itself, forcing the divine blood to collapse into ash and absence. Pain tears through you, white-hot and absolute, as the storm howls above, robbed of its chosen path. The sky fractures, then recoils, its voice breaking into dissonance as the godborn current unravels. When the Chorus finally falls silent, you are left standing amid the aftermath, alive, perhaps, but forever altered by what you have destroyed. Step onto The Unseen Age on page 270.

# Chapter 19
## The Quiet Vein

THE PAIN DOES NOT linger the way you expect it to. When the Ancestral Thread tears free, it burns bright and brief, a flash of white that steals breath and thought alike. Then it is gone, not dulled. Not sleeping. Gone. In its absence, there is no echoing scream, no divine reprisal, no answering thunder. Only a sudden, profound quiet that settles behind your eyes, like a room emptied after a long vigil. You sway. Cairenn's hut smells sharply of smoke and bone and something bitter you cannot name. The lineage-sticks hanging from the rafters sway as well, though no wind touches them now. Cairenn watches you with an expression neither shocked nor relieved—only weary, as if witnessing the final note of a song they have heard too many times to mourn properly. "It is done," they murmur. Not as blessing. Not as condemnation. As fact.

You wait for the storm's attention to snap back into focus. For that intimate pressure you have come to recognize—the sense of being weighed, measured, found useful. It does not return. Somewhere far above the hills, thunder rolls, but it is distant, un-focused. Weather, not witness. The coiled knot beneath your skin has faded to a pale scar, warm but inert. You press your fin-gers to it, half-expecting pain, half-expect-ing it to pulse back to life. It does neither. Cairenn exhales slowly. "The vein has gone quiet," they say. "Not sealed. Not healed. Simply no longer carrying what it once did."

Outside, the hills look unchanged. Grass bends in the wind. Clouds move with fa-miliar indifference. The world has not end-ed. That, somehow, unsettles you more than catastrophe would have. You leave the bone-hut at dawn. No spirits bar your way. No ancestral voices trail behind you. The path feels lighter beneath your feet, as though some unseen weight has lift-ed—not only from you, but from the land itself. You are alone now in a way you have never been before. Mortal in the fullest sense. Finite. Unwatched. At first, the changes are subtle. Seers begin to argue more often. Their visions disagree. Omens fail to align. A druid's reading of smoke contradicts another's dream. Storms come without pattern, without warning, without message. People still pray. Still leave offerings. But the answers arrive late, if at all, and never quite match what was asked.

Years pass. Shrines fall into disrepair. Not violently—no lightning strikes them down—but through neglect. Roofs leak. Carvings soften beneath rain. The old rituals are still performed, but more out of habit than necessity. They become festivals rather than safeguards, stories rather than instructions. Children are taught the old myths, then taught how to test them. Why does the river flood? Why does the fever spread? Why does the sky darken before rain?

Answers emerge that do not require sacrifice. Observation replaces invocation. Record replaces revelation. The druids who once spoke with spirits begin to write instead—marking patterns, measuring seasons, comparing outcomes. They are uneasy at first, as if committing a quiet heresy, but the results speak with a clarity the gods have long abandoned.

Cairenn fades from memory. Not abruptly. Not cruelly. Simply without audience. Fewer come to ask about bloodlines. Fewer care which ancestor once carried thunder in their veins. The bone-hut remains, but it is visited by scholars rather than supplicants, its relics catalogued, its stories preserved as history rather than prophecy. Storms become storms. They still devastate. Still kill. But they no longer feel intentional. No one speaks of godborn tempests or listening skies. Instead, people build stronger roofs. Dig better channels. Learn where not to settle. Loss becomes tragedy rather than judgment.

Generations pass. Tools improve—healing advances. A child who would once have died of fever survives because someone learned to boil water, to isolate sickness, to test remedies rather than pray them away. Knowledge spreads unevenly at first, then faster, carried by trade rather than omen.

The world grows louder. Not with divine voices—but with human ones.

Debate replaces prophecy. Councils replace oracles. There are mistakes, terrible ones. Some failures would have once been softened by myth or explained away by fate. Now they are faced directly. Blame is argued. Responsibility is assigned. Sometimes unjustly. Sometimes with painful clarity.

You do not see this age. You live out your mortal span quietly. You are remembered for a time as the Seer Who Walked Away, though even that title fades, softened into footnote, then speculation. Did you truly sever the thread? Or was magic always waning? Scholars argue. Priests protest. No one can prove either side. And the storm never corrects them.

By the time centuries have passed, the gods are stories told with affection or skepticism, depending on the teller. Prophecy becomes metaphor. Magic becomes folklore. The world is no longer shaped by what might be destined, but by what is attempted, refined, corrected, or endured. Ériu is no longer guided. It is responsible. And so it reaches a turning point—not marked by lightning or omen, but by scale. Humanity now holds tools powerful enough to heal across borders or destroy beyond imagining. With no gods to judge, no prophecy to warn, the direction taken will be entirely its own. History pauses here, pen lifted, waiting for what comes next.

The unguided world has two possible paths. Two possible futures. People will make this choice, and people will complete the story. Which ending would you like to see for your adventure?

A. The world turns toward shared knowledge and care: Communities choose cooperation over conquest, building systems that value life, learning, and mutual survival. Medicine spreads faster than armies. Borders soften where necessity demands unity. Progress is uneven, imperfect—but driven by responsibility rather than fear of divine wrath. The story ends in The Age of Hands and Minds on page 189.

B. The world replaces gods with crowns and cannons. Power consolidates. Technology advances without restraint. One ruler follows another, each promising order while delivering devastation. With no prophecy to contradict them, authority goes unchecked, and disaster becomes man-made and relentless. The sky remains silent—not merciful, not cruel. Simply absent. Complete your adventure at The Iron Crown on page 229.

# Chapter 20
# The Unbound Tempest

THE STORM BREAKS ITS patience. It does not erupt in blind fury. It hunts. Lightning strikes the place where you stood moments earlier, splitting the earth with surgical precision. The air screams as thunder crashes without pause, one concussion layered atop the next, as though the sky has forgotten how to inhale. Wind tears through the land in violent, directional bursts—trees ripped from the ground and hurled aside, roofs lifted and scattered like chaff. You run. Not in panic. Not in denial. In grim clarity.

You understand now what refusal has done. The storm did not hear defiance as rejection—it heard release. By denying it communion, you stripped away restraint, severed the last tether that encouraged patience, dialogue, and balance. The godborn force no longer seeks understanding. It seeks completion.

Rain lashes sideways, sharp as thrown gravel. Each breath burns your lungs, charged with ozone and debris. The ground bucks beneath your feet, cracks opening and closing as if the land itself cannot decide whether to flee or stand. Somewhere behind you, a village bell rings once—then is swallowed by thunder and collapse. People scatter in every direction. You glimpse them briefly through sheets of rain—figures bent low, clutching children, dragging the elderly, abandoning homes without a backward glance. Screams vanish into the storm's roar. Fires ignite and are extinguished in the same breath, smoke torn apart before it can rise.

This is not punishment. This is indifference given motion. The storm moves with intent now, its center shifting to keep you always just ahead of devastation. Lightning arcs not randomly, but in narrowing patterns, herding you forward. Each time you change direction, the wind adjusts instantly, correcting, tightening the chase. Your body aches with exhaustion and strain. Your legs burn—your vision blurs at the edges. Still, you run, because stopping would mean surrendering to a force that has no concept of mercy.

Memory surfaces unbidden as you flee. Old teachings. Half-forgotten warnings. Stories of storms that did not disperse, but consumed. Of druids who stood against them and were erased so completely that their names dissolved from record. Of one place—spoken of rarely, never lightly—where storms once ended not by spreading, but by collapsing inward.

A convergence site. An ancient scar in the land where pressure folds upon itself, where sky and earth refuse to carry excess force any farther. If storms die anywhere, they die there. The knowledge sharpens into purpose. You change course. The storm notices immediately. Wind howls louder, pressing against your back with crushing force. Lightning slams into the ground ahead, forcing you to veer sharply to avoid a widening fissure that glows briefly with subterranean fire. Rain thickens into sheets so dense the world narrows to a few desperate strides at a time.

The land rises unevenly as you approach the convergence site, broken stone and exposed bedrock jutting upward like bones. Ancient markers—long toppled, their runes worn smooth—dot the path, remnants of rites abandoned when the cost became too high. You stumble. Fall. Scramble back to your feet as thunder detonates so close that your vision whites out entirely. For a moment, you cannot hear anything at all. Then sound returns all at once—wind, rain, thunder layered so thick it becomes almost solid. You taste blood. You do not know if it is yours.

Ahead, the convergence site reveals itself. A wide basin carved into the land, ringed by fractured stone pillars fused at their edges by long-past lightning strikes. The air above it twists violently, pressure collapsing inward rather than expanding outward. You feel it immediately—the storm's momentum stuttering, confused by a place that refuses to let force pass unchallenged. The storm roars. Not in anger.

In recognition. This place can end it, or trap it long enough to choose another path.

Another understanding cuts through your exhaustion—quiet, unwelcome, undeniable. This basin does not destroy storms. It never has. It breaks them apart. You feel it now in the way pressure pulls downward instead of outward, how force refuses to pass cleanly through this place. The land here does not repel excess power—it absorbs it, fractures it, scatters it into veins of stone and soil that lead far beyond the horizon. This was never meant to be a weapon. It was a release. A way for the sky's burden to be shared by the world rather than carried by one will alone.

You stagger into the basin's edge, boots skidding on slick stone. The wind claws at you from all sides, trying to lift you, slam you, tear you apart. Lightning lashes downward, striking the pillars again and again, seeking purchase. Your strength is nearly gone. And still another realization rises, cold and unavoidable. You are not required to fight the storm. You could ride it.

You now understand how its movement works and how its pressure seeks paths of least resistance. If you surrender to that flow—not submitting, but aligning—you might survive. You could guide destruction just enough to avoid your own end, letting the storm burn itself across the land while you remain standing in its wake. You would live. The cost would be measured in scorched villages, drowned fields, broken lives. The land would remember what passed through it—and who did not stop it. The storm tightens overhead, lightning splitting the sky open in jagged seams. The basin hums violently, struggling to contain what presses against it. Your muscles shake with fatigue—your vision swims. There will be no second chance. This decision must be made now. You draw a breath thick with rain and ash.

A. You plant your feet at the heart of the basin and brace yourself, forcing your body to become anchor and shield. The storm crashes against you in waves of unbearable pressure, tearing at flesh, bone, and will alike. Survival is uncertain, but the land behind you is spared the worst of what follows. With conviction, you face The Tragic Stand on page 159.

B.     You choose to break the storm into the land itself. You recognize the truth too late for fear to matter: this place was never meant to end storms—only to stop them from remaining whole. Instead of bracing or fleeing, you drive your will downward, forcing the storm's gathered force to fracture and sink into the land beneath your feet. The basin screams as pressure collapses inward, then outward, splintering the godborn tempest into a thousand unseen currents that race through soil, stone, and root alike. Lightning does not strike again—it dissolves, bleeding into the earth in blinding threads that vanish as quickly as they form. You are thrown hard against the ground, breath torn from your lungs, as the sky above clears in ragged, uneven patches. When you rise, the storm is gone—but the land hums beneath your palms, awake in ways it has not been for generations. Proceed to The Awakened Land on page 288.

# Chapter 21
## The Fractured Dominion

THE BINDING LOCKS. NOT cleanly. Not kindly. It locks the way bone knits under pressure—warped, rigid, screaming beneath the surface. When you carve the final reinforcing sigil, the stone beneath your feet splits with a sound like a great tree breaking in winter. Light flares upward, white-hot and blinding, and for a heartbeat you think the storm has torn free after all. Then everything stills.

The wind dies as if strangled. Lightning freezes into jagged veins across the sky, unmoving, unreal. The thunder does not fade—it halts, cut off mid-roar, leaving a silence so dense it presses against your ears. You are on your knees again, palms braced against scorched stone, breath coming in shallow, ragged pulls. Every muscle trembles as though you have lifted something far heavier than your body was meant to bear.

The storm is bound. And it is furious. You feel it immediately—not as sound or image, but as constant pressure inside your skull, behind your eyes, beneath your skin. The storm no longer exists above you alone. It has nowhere else to go. It presses into you. The sigils burn steadily now, no longer flickering, their light sharp and contained. The ritual circle hums with strained stability, vibrating like a taut wire pulled too tight. Cracks race outward from the center, carving fault lines through the upland stone. Far below, Ériu reacts.

You feel it through the binding as if through stretched nerves: weather stalling unnaturally, clouds piling without release, winds curling into tight, localized spirals that scour fields and coastlines without moving on. Storms no longer travel. They collect. Where you stand becomes a center. A dominion.

You rise slowly, spine screaming in protest, and the world rises with you. The frozen lightning above shifts, not striking, not dispersing—orbiting. The storm has been forced into a shape it never wore before: compressed, constrained, focused. Controlled. The realization chills you more than the silence.

You walk. The storm moves with you. Not willingly—but inevitably, dragged by the binding etched into stone, blood, and will. Wherever you pause too long, the air thickens. The ground darkens. Rain threatens but never quite falls. People sense it before they see it, stepping aside as animals do when the weather turns wrong.

Villages whisper your passing into new names. Stormwarden. Binder. Walking Tempest. Some greet you with reverence. Others with fear sharp enough to taste. A few with relief—because where you linger, storms do not strike. The violence is held, bottled, restrained. At a terrible cost. Days pass. Weeks. The pressure inside you does not lessen. It accumulates.

You learn quickly what the binding demands. Rest becomes shallow. Sleep fractures into flashes of thunderless lightning behind closed eyes. Your breath syncs unconsciously with the storm's rhythm, and when your heart races, clouds tighten overhead. You are no longer merely carrying the storm. You are regulating it.

Druin finds you at the edge of a shattered plain where grass has been flattened into glassy black sheets by repeated, localized strikes. He stops several paces away, wary, as if approaching a wild thing that might lash out without warning. "You did it," he says. Not accusation. Not praise. Statement. "I contained it," you reply. Your voice sounds wrong to your own ears—too steady, too resonant. "For how long?" he asks. You do not answer immediately. The truth presses hard against your ribs. "I don't know," you admit at last. "But it won't break free easily."

Druin studies the sky above you—the frozen arcs of lightning, the way the clouds curve inward, disciplined and tense. His jaw tightens. "It's not free," he says. "It's trapped." "Yes." "And traps," he continues carefully, "are not meant to last forever." As if summoned by the words, a tremor ripples through the air. The sigils etched into distant stone flare faintly. Pain lances through your temples, sharp enough to steal breath. You stagger. Druin steps forward instinctively, then stops, realizing too late what crossing closer might mean.

The storm surges against the binding. Not blindly. Not violently. Testing. It finds the weakest seam—not in the stone, not in the sigils, but in you. Memory fractures first. You lose small things: a name here, a face there. Moments slip loose, replaced by raw sensation—pressure, movement, force. Your thoughts begin to align along unfamiliar pathways, prioritizing balance and containment over empathy or fear. You are becoming an instrument.

People begin to gather around you—not in rebellion, but in dependence. They ask you to stay. To linger near fields during harvest. To stand watch over coastlines when storms threaten to break free. Each request makes sense. Each is reasonable. Each tightens the compression.

The storm responds obediently, contained, reshaped into a localized presence that does not wander. But the land around you begins to suffer under the unnatural focus. Soil near your path hardens. Rivers hesitate. Birds avoid the sky entirely, skirting low and wide around your wake. You feel it all. Every imbalance registers inside your chest like an unstruck note begging for release. One night, the binding nearly fails.

You wake choking on lightning that has no sound, your body arched as if struck. The sky above convulses, the frozen arcs shuddering violently. The sigils flare so bright you see them through closed eyes. Druin is there when you collapse, shouting your name as the ground cracks open beneath your feet. "You can't keep this up!" he yells, bracing himself against the shockwaves rippling outward. "The storm is eating you alive!" You know he is right. The binding was never meant to be held externally forever. It demands a release, a resolution. Something must change—soon.

You retreat to the original ritual ground, dragging the storm with you like a chained beast. The stone circle groans under the pressure of its return. The air bends visibly now, shimmering as if heat-warped. You have reached the edge of what control can sustain. There are only two paths left.

You can shatter the binding deliberately—release the storm in a single, catastrophic purge that will tear the ritual apart and scar the land, but end the compression once and for all. You might survive. You might not. But the storm would be free. Or you can do the unthinkable. You can internalize the binding completely—pull the sigils, the pressure, the containment into yourself. Become the living seal. A prison of flesh and will strong enough to hold what stone cannot. You understand the cost instantly. One choice ends the storm's captivity in fire and ruin. The other ends you—slowly, completely, permanently. The storm presses harder, sensing decision. The land holds its breath.

A. You sacrifice the binding. You tear the sigils apart, unleashing the storm in a final, violent release. Lightning screams free, the sky breaking open as centuries of compressed force explode outward. The ritual shatters—and with it, your hold on the storm. Whether you survive the cleansing destruction remains uncertain. You move to The Storm's Release on page 166.

B. You become the living seal. You draw the binding inward, carving the sigils into flesh, memory, and soul. The storm collapses into you, imprisoned by will alone. The land stabilizes as you stand immobile, eternal and unyielding—the storm's cage and warning made flesh. You find your way as The Living Cataclysm, page 214.

# Chapter 22
# The Land Without Kings

THE CHANGE BEGINS BEFORE anyone names it. It moves faster than rumor, faster than riders. It moves the way weather moves—felt first in the bones, in the breath, in the way animals lift their heads and decide to leave familiar ground. When you step back into the open air from beneath the hall, Tara does not greet you as it did before. The hill is awake. Not stirring—awake.

The Lia Fáil does not cry out, but it hums, a low vibration that trembles through soil and stone. The standing stones ring the hilltop with a new tension, their old cracks faintly luminous, no longer wounds but mouths opened after long silence. The sky hangs low, gray and watchful, not storming, not calm. Waiting.

Inside the hall, Maelchon's laughter falters. You hear it break off mid-sentence, sharp as a snapped thread. Then voices rise—confusion first, then anger—cups tip. Benches scrape. Somewhere, a blade leaves its sheath. The land has spoken.

It does not declare a new ruler. It does not elevate you. It does not name anyone king. Instead, it withdraws something that has been given for too long without consent. Acceptance. You feel it ripple outward, a vast refusal. Fields that once yielded easily turn stubborn. Hearth-fires gutter unless tended with care. Oaths spoken without truth carry no weight at all. Men who have ruled by inherited certainty wake with the sensation that the ground beneath their feet is no longer listening.

Druin emerges beside you, pale, eyes reflecting the standing stones like shards of moonlight. "It's begun," he says, though there is no triumph in his voice. Only awe and fear braided together. Below the hill, the hall erupts.

Maelchon stumbles from his seat as if struck. He does not fall—but he sways, one hand gripping the arm of the throne, the other pressing to his chest. His crown slides further askew, no longer merely symbolic. He looks suddenly smaller, as though the air itself has decided not to hold him up anymore.

"What have you done?" someone shouts. Not at you. At the world. A warrior kneels, unbidden, gasping as though the stone floor has grown too heavy beneath his knees. Another laughs, hysterical, then stops when the sound echoes back wrong, hollow. Druids rush forward, hands raised—not in blessing, but in instinctive warding. They feel it too: the old law stretching its limbs, testing the edges of its long confinement.

Maelchon's gaze finds you through the open doors. For a moment, hatred flares. Then something worse replaces it. Understanding. "You've undone us," he says hoarsely. "There is no order without kings." The land answers him—not with words, but with a tremor that runs through the hill. Dust shakes loose from the beams. The Lia Fáil hum deepens, steady and unmoved by his fear. "Order," the land seems to say, "was never yours to keep."

People scatter from Tara before sunset. Some flee in terror, convinced the world has ended. Others leave with relief they cannot explain, as if a pressure they had lived under since birth has lifted. Messengers ride hard in every direction, carrying news that sounds like madness: the land has withdrawn its blessing. Some kings barricade themselves in halls and fortresses. Some kneel in fields and beg forgiveness from soil that does not answer easily.

Within days, borders blur. Old rivalries flare without the thin restraint of crowned authority. Some villages dissolve into argument. Others gather in circles and speak until dawn, choosing leaders by voice, by memory, by who listens best. In a few places, violence erupts—unchecked, confused, desperate.

You walk among it all like a fault line given form. Where you step, the ground steadies. Not because you command it, but because it recognizes the choice that was made through you. The land does not obey you—but it does not push you away.

Druin remains at your side longer than anyone else. "You've given them freedom," he says one night as you stand overlooking a valley where fires burn without banners. "And you've taken away the lie that held them together." "They will adapt," you answer, though uncertainty threads your voice. "They always have." He studies you carefully. "The land will adapt. People may not." The truth of that settles heavily.

Without kings, Ériu is raw. Honest. Dangerous. The land no longer cushions poor decisions. It does not smooth over cruelty with ceremony. When leaders arise, they must earn the ground beneath them every day—or lose it. And still something is missing.

You feel it when you stand alone at dawn. The law beneath stone has been restored enough to free the land—but it is not whole. The old system had balances, rituals, and bindings that prevented chaos from hardening into endless bloodshed. Kings abused those structures—but they existed for a reason. Now there is a void where authority once sat.

A void does not remain empty. Druin voices what others dare not. "If nothing replaces the crown," he says quietly, "someone worse will." You feel the land listening again—not demanding, but attentive. It does not choose rulers anymore. But it is willing to accept law if law is shaped with care.

You could step back. Let Ériu decide its own order in fits and starts. Let villages rise and fall, leaders tested and replaced, violence burn itself out where it must. The land would heal wild and uneven, scarred but alive. No single hand would guide it—but no single hand would strangle it either.

Or you could act again. You could impose a new sacred law—not kingship reborn, but something colder, firmer. A binding code etched into stone and soil alike. One that defines leadership, punishment, and inheritance. One that prevents chaos by force of permanence. The land would accept it if you anchor it deeply enough. But such law would not listen once set. And neither, perhaps, would you.

The storm stirs far above—not raging, not gone. Watching and measuring what kind of order might emerge in the space that the kings once occupied. Druin does not tell you what to choose. He only asks one question, voice barely above the wind. "Do you trust the land to heal itself," he says, "or only yourself to decide how it should be shaped?"

You stand at the edge of the hill and look out over Ériu without crowns. Fires flicker. Voices rise. Paths diverge. The land waits—not for a king, but for a decision.

A. You let the land choose its own order. You step back and refuse to shape what must grow wild. You allow communities to rise, fail, and rise again without a single law binding them all. The land responds slowly, unevenly, but honestly—renewing itself through trial and memory rather than decree. There will be suffering. There will be beauty. Ériu will never again belong to one voice alone. Proceed on your adventure with Wild Renewal on page 180.

B. You impose a new sacred law. You carve authority back into the world—not as a crown, but as a binding law that answers to no ruler but itself. The land accepts the structure, locking it into stone and soil, and chaos retreats beneath enforced order. Stability returns swiftly—but at the cost of flexibility, mercy, and dissent. You become the architect of permanence, and Ériu becomes shaped to endure you. And now you must face the Tyranny of Sacred Law on page 199.

# Chapter 23
## The Path of Reckoning

THE BOG RELEASES YOU slowly. Not all at once, not willingly, but inch by inch, as if it must be certain you will not try to take anything more from it. Cold water slips from your boots. Mud loosens its grip on your calves. The mist thins behind you, though the sound of sighing follows for a long while, breaths finally exhaled by things that have waited too long. You emerge onto firmer ground shaken, hollowed, and lighter in a way that frightens you.

The confession you offered the Bog-Warden still rings in your bones. Words spoken aloud that cannot be pulled back. Truths named that now exist in the world, no longer locked inside fear or silence. You feel exposed, as though your skin has been peeled back and the land has looked directly at what lies beneath. Behind you, the Bog-Warden sinks once more into dark water, its voice fading as a bell lowered into depth. "Go. And do not pretend you were never weighed." You do not look back.

The path forward is narrow, rising gently out of the low ground. Each step feels deliberate, as though the land itself is testing your resolve. The sky above remains heavy with storm, but the thunder has changed. It no longer prowls. It listens.

You walk for hours, perhaps days. Time stretches, elastic and strange, until you crest a rise and see Tara again. The Hill of Tara stands unchanged at first glance—mist-wrapped, ringed by stones—but as you draw closer, you sense the difference immediately. The cracks in the standing stones glow faintly, not with silver lightning, but with a warmer hue, like embers cooling after fire. The Rune-Shard (Tara) at your side hums softly, then stills.

The land is waiting. You climb the hill alone. No ravens circle now. No ancestors whisper. The silence feels earned rather than ominous. When you step into the ring of stones, the Lia Fáil greets you with a low vibration that travels up through your feet into your chest. You kneel, not because you must, but because standing feels wrong here.

The confession you made in the bog has already begun to work. You feel it in the way the air steadies, in the way the storm clouds hesitate rather than tighten. The godborn storm is still present—vast, unfinished—but it no longer surges blindly. It is being held. Not by force. By truth.

You rise and move to the Lia Fáil. The great crack down its face remains, but it has not widened. Instead, the edges look cleaner as if the stone has accepted the wound rather than fighting it. You place your palm against the stone. It is cool. Solid. Present. No vision overwhelms you this time. No voice declares destiny. Instead, something subtler happens: the land listens back.

You speak—not loudly, not ritually, but honestly. You speak the truth you named in the bog: about the false crown, about the storm born of fractured prophecy, about your refusal to become its vessel or its master. You speak of fear. You speak of limits. You speak of choosing repair over dominion. The words are not perfect. They do not need to be. As the last syllable leaves your mouth, the ground trembles—once, gently. The storm responds. Not with lightning. With rain.

The first drops fall hesitantly, leaving soft, darkened marks on the grass. The smell of earth rises—rich, grounding, real. You lift your face and let the rain soak your hair, your cloak, your skin. Above, the clouds loosen. Far out over Ériu, thunder rolls, not as a threat, but as retreat. The godborn storm does not vanish. It does not collapse. It recedes, its vast shape thinning, its pressure easing, as though deprived of the sharp edges it needed to finish forming. Without lies to sharpen it, without buried truths to feed it, it cannot complete itself. It drifts upward and away, unfinished and unwilling. A presence lingers briefly—vast, disappointed, contemplative. Then it is gone.

You remain. The stones of Tara settle. One by one, the glowing cracks dim until they are only stone again, bearing scars that will not vanish but will not worsen. Scars, you realize, are not always signs of failure. They are records. Days pass.

Word spreads—not in a single dramatic wave, but in careful ripples. The king's authority weakens as people speak aloud what they once only whispered. Maelchon's reign does not end in fire or blood. It ends in quiet erosion. The land no longer answers him. The Lia Fáil remains silent beneath his feet. He abdicates before winter.

No new crown cries out to claim the throne. And that, too, is a kind of healing. You do not take power. No one offers it—not truly. Instead, they come to you with questions. With disputes. With fears about what comes next when gods do not rule, and kings must answer to the land again. You answer when you can. When you cannot, you say so. You travel Ériu in the months that follow, not as ruler or prophet, but as witness. You help rebind old oaths in new words. You listen to villages argue their way toward fairness. You remind kings that the land listens longer than they live.

The relics you carried change. The Oath-Stone Fragment cools and fractures naturally, becoming an ordinary stone once more. Its purpose fulfilled. The Rune-Shard (Tara) loses its hum, settling into stillness. You bury it beneath the hill, where it belongs, not as a weapon or key, but as memory returned to stone. Even the marks on your skin fade, not erased, but absorbed, becoming part of you rather than signs upon you.

Years later, how many, you cannot say, you return to Tara at dawn. Mist curls softly around the stones. Grass bends beneath your steps. The Lia Fáil stands silent, scarred, enduring. You sit among the stones and watch the sky lighten.

No storm gathers. And for the first time since the prophecy cracked, you feel no pull toward destiny. Only presence. Only breath. Only land. You are not remembered as a god. You are not sung of as a king. But when storms come to Ériu in later years, they break cleanly and pass. The land holds. The stones do not crack again. And somewhere beneath Tara, buried deep and quiet, prophecy rests, no longer hidden, no longer weaponized. Simply known.

# Chapter 24
# The Lingering Curse

THE BOG DOES NOT release you the way a river releases a leaf. It releases you the way a hand releases a throat—slowly, reluctantly, with the memory of pressure still stamped into flesh. You stumble out of the Bog of Sighs with mud clinging to your boots and cold water dripping from your hem in steady threads. The air beyond the bog is clearer, almost sweet, yet your lungs do not fill easily. Each breath feels borrowed, as if the bog still owns a portion of it. Behind you, the mist coils, folding back over dark water like a lid closing.

The Bog-Warden has accepted what you offered. It did not reject you. It did not drag you down. It did not roar its displeasure. That is what unsettles you most. Because the bog did not hunger the way it should have. It simply weighed you, took what you gave, and decided it was enough to let you pass—enough for now.

The Warden's voice still clings to the inside of your skull like damp reed-fiber: "A partial truth is still an oath broken. Go, Seer. The rest will follow you."

You walk faster as the ground firms beneath you, as if speed might outrun meaning. You push uphill through thickets of gorse and hawthorn, ignoring the scratches on your hands, ignoring the tug in your calves. Yet the farther you get from the bog, the more certain you become of something impossible: The sound of sighing is still behind you. Not loud. Not constant. But present—like breath near your ear when you are alone. You stop on the path and turn.

The world behind you is ordinary: gray sky, pale grass, a distant smear of mist where the bog lies. No figure rises. No hollow eyes watch from the water. No hands reach up. And yet a thin ribbon of fog drifts across the ground toward your feet, against the wind. It touches your boot. And the cold of it is not the cold of water. It is the cold of a promise that has not been kept. You swallow and continue.

By late day, you reach the first scattered farms at the edge of Tara's lands. Smoke rises from chimneys—sheep bleat. A dog barks at your approach—then abruptly falls silent, ears flattening as if it hears something you cannot. A woman at a fence looks up from tying rushes. Her gaze fixes on you, and her face drains of color. Not fear of a stranger. Not suspicion of a druid. Recognition.

"Seer…" she whispers. Then, softer, as if to herself: "No. Not you. Not now." You step closer. "What is it?" She backs away, eyes wide. "There's wet on you," she says. "Not mud. Not rain. Wet that shouldn't be here." You glance down. Your cloak is damp from the bog, yes—but that is not what she means. The way she stares is too precise, as if she sees a stain that does not show to mortal sight. You follow her gaze to your shadow. For an instant, your shadow looks wrong. It does not sit at your feet as it should. It stretches a fraction longer. It shivers at the edges. And within it, faint as a dying ember, is the shape of a mouth opening in silent breath.

The woman crosses herself with a hurried charm-gesture and flees into her house, slamming the door hard enough to startle birds from a nearby hedge. A thin laugh, wet, quiet, threads through the air behind you. You whip around. Nothing. But the grass near your heels is flattened as if something passed close, something low and patient—your Fate Mark prickles. The Rune-Shard (Tara) in your pouch hums once, uneasily, then falls silent again—as if it does not wish to draw attention.

You walk on, forcing your steps steady, forcing your breathing slow. If you can reach Tara, you tell yourself, you can set this right. You can place your hands to the stone. You can speak what you did not speak in the bog. You can—

A sigh brushes your ear, intimate as breath. You flinch so hard you nearly stumble. A whisper follows the sigh, and this time it is not the ancestors. It is not the storm. It is the Bog. "Not yet." Night falls before you reach the hill.

Clouds mass overhead, not as tightly coiled as before—no great spiral, no towering humanoid shape—but heavy enough to press down on your thoughts. The moon shows only as a pale blur.

You take shelter beneath an old oak, its roots thick and exposed like knuckles gripping earth. You build a small fire. The flames catch reluctantly, as if the wood itself is unsure whether it should burn in your presence. The moment the fire stabilizes, you feel it: a dampness at the edge of the circle of light, just beyond where the glow fades into darkness. You hold still. Listen.

A single slow drip falls from a branch overhead, though the branch is dry. Another drip. Then another. A rhythm forms, patient as a heartbeat. Your skin tightens. You look up and see nothing. Yet the dripping continues. You stare at the ground where the drops land. The soil darkens in small spots. And in each darkened spot, a tiny bubble rises—like breath coming up from deep water. The bubbles pop soundlessly. The sighing grows stronger—your fire flickers.

You reach for the Oath-Stone Fragment—if you still carry it—and find it colder than it should be, as if it has been submerged. Your own breath fogs the air, though the night is not that cold. You whisper into the darkness, voice low. "I paid the bog. I gave what was asked." The air behind you shifts. A shape forms at the edge of the firelight, tall, thin, draped in mist. Not fully the Bog-Warden. Not fully anything. A portion. A remainder. A debt with legs. It does not step into the light. It does not need to. Its presence alone leans in like weight. "You gave what you chose to give," it whispers. "Not what was owed." Your mouth goes dry. "I confessed." "Partly." The word is wet. "And what is partly spoken is partly bound. That is the curse of half-truths: they must be completed, or they complete you."

The fire dims, as if frightened. You force yourself upright, keeping your posture steady. You have stood before kings. You have stood under lightning. You will not crouch before a thing born of drowned oaths. "What do you want?" you ask. The mist-shape tilts, almost amused. "Not want. Weight. Carry it." And suddenly you understand.

The curse is not a wound you can treat with herbs or prayer. It is a burden of unfinished truth, a thing that will follow you until the withheld words are spoken—or until it consumes the spaces where words should be. It will twist your shadow. It will sour your presence. It will turn your silence into a beacon for the storm, because storms love fractures. You feel panic claw at your ribs. You swallow it down hard. "Then I will speak," you say. "At Tara. I will—" The mist-shape's whisper interrupts, soft and cruel. "Not there." You freeze. "Why?" "Because Tara is stone. Tara remembers. Tara judges. If you speak at Tara, the hill will decide what your truth costs."

The fire collapses inward, shrinking to a tight knot of flame. In the dim light, you see your shadow shift again—longer, thinner—and in it, the faint mouth opens wider, as if inhaling. The bog's remainder leans closer, still not fully visible, still not fully here. "You will try to restore prophecy, Seer. You will gather fragments. You will bargain with gods and men. But every time you choose silence when truth is required. I will grow, and when I am whole, you will no longer be able to speak at all." Your heart hammers. A life without speech is more than death for a Seer. Without speech, you cannot bind oaths. You cannot complete rites. You cannot name a thing, and in the old laws, what cannot be named cannot be contained. The storm wants unfinished things. The bog wants debts paid. And you stand between them, marked as a walking fracture.

Dawn comes gray and thin. When you rise, the oak's roots are wet, though no rain has fallen. Your fire is ash. Your throat feels rough, as if you spoke all night. You did not. As you begin the final climb toward Tara, you catch sight of your reflection in a puddle along the path. Your face is yours. But behind your eyes, something looks damp—a sheen, like water caught on glass. You blink. It remains.

At the hill's crest, the standing stones emerge from the mist like teeth. They are still cracked. They are still waiting. And the storm above is still present—not fully formed, not entirely gone—hovering like a decision postponed. You step into the ring. The Lia Fáil stands before you, its great fissure glowing faintly. When you approach, the stone does not brighten in welcome. It grows colder. The air thickens. The hill senses the curse on you. The Ancestral Chorus stirs faintly, uneasy. What have you brought back? They whisper.

You reach out, palm hovering just above the stone. This is the moment to speak what you withheld. To complete the truth. To pay the debt. But fear tightens, because you now understand what the bog meant: Speaking here will not merely cleanse you. It will cost you. A relic. A future path. A person's life. Your own. The Lia Fáil's crack pulses once, like a heartbeat. Your shadow stretches behind you, and the mouth within it opens, waiting to drink whatever you choose not to say. You draw breath.

A. You feel the weight of what you withheld press heavier with every step toward the hill, the curse tightening as if resisting its own ending. When you finally speak the truth aloud—fully, without trimming or mercy—the land responds at once, shuddering as buried oaths resurface. The mark burns, then fractures, its power unraveling in a surge that leaves you reeling and exposed. Relief follows, but it is not gentle; Tara does not forgive without balance. Something must be surrendered in return—status, memory, protection, or future claim. You remain alive and unclaimed, but the ground beneath you will never feel entirely steady again. Complete your adventure with The Silent Balance on page 145.

B. You turn away from Tara, letting silence close over what was never fully confessed. The curse does not resist—it settles, deepening into something deliberate and patient, reshaping itself around your will. Power answers more readily now, sharp and precise, no longer burdened by hesitation. The mark ceases to ache and begins to instruct, offering leverage where honesty would have demanded sacrifice. Somewhere above, within cloud and pressure, the storm becomes aware of the choice you have made. You are no longer merely followed by consequence—you are being measured for dominion. Go to Crown of Ruin on page 173.

# Chapter 25
## The Silent Balance

THE HILL OF TARA receives you without welcome. Mist coils low around the stones, muffling sound, blunting distance. The standing pillars rise like patient judges who have already heard too many confessions to be surprised by another. The crack in the Lia Fáil glows faintly, not with silver fire or storm-light, but with a dull, inward gleam, like an eye that has chosen not to blink. You step into the ring, and the ground tightens beneath your boots. Not hostility. Containment.

The curse you carry shifts within you, restless. The damp pressure of the bog lingers behind your eyes, in your throat, in the lengthening edge of your shadow. It does not urge you to speak. It urges you to wait—to let silence do what silence always does. The Ancestral Chorus stirs faintly, uneasy. You return unfinished, they whisper. And yet you stand.

You stop before the Lia Fáil. The air smells of cold stone and old rain. When you lift your hand, it trembles—not from fear, but from the knowledge that this is a moment the land will remember even if no one else does. You could speak everything now. You could tear the last veil away and let Tara decide the price. You feel the weight of that choice pressing down like a blade balanced on breath. But you also feel something else. Control.

You have learned the shape of the storm. You have seen how prophecy fractures into weapons when spoken without care. You now understand that truth not only heals—it destabilizes. It tears down structures faster than they can be rebuilt. Ériu is tired. You are tired. You lower your hand. "I will not speak it all," you say quietly—not as defiance, but as decision. "Not yet." The Lia Fáil does not crack further. That is the first sign.

The glow within its fissure dims slightly, as if the stone itself exhales. The ground beneath your feet steadies, no longer quivering on the edge of judgment. The storm above hesitates—its pressure easing, its form loosening. The curse inside you tightens once, testing the boundary—then settles. It understands restraint. A low vibration runs through the ring of stones. Not approval. Not condemnation. Acceptance. The Ancestral Chorus withdraws, their whispers thinning like breath in cold air. "Balance," they murmur. "Held. Not healed."

You step back from the stone, and the hill allows it. The days that follow pass without catastrophe. The storm does not complete itself. It remains present—distant thunder, restless clouds—but it no longer sharpens toward violence. Crops survive. Rivers stay within their banks. Ériu endures, not renewed, but intact. Word spreads cautiously. The king's authority weakens, but does not collapse. Maelchon remains on his throne, though the Lia Fáil never answers him again. He rules carefully now, wary of every oath he speaks. Fear tempers his excesses more effectively than truth ever did. You do not challenge him again. Nor does he challenge you—instead, a quiet understanding forms—unspoken, uneasy. You are allowed to travel. To mediate disputes. To advise, when asked. You are never named ruler and never crowned. But your presence becomes a stabilizing force, a reminder of consequences not fully enacted.

Some call you wise. Others call you dangerous. Both are correct. The curse does not leave you. It does not worsen either. It becomes contained. You learn its boundaries. Learn how to keep your voice steady when truth presses against your teeth. Learn how to redirect conversations away from fractures that would widen too quickly. Learn when silence preserves more than speech would destroy. Your shadow never quite shortens. On certain nights, when fog is thick and the moon thin, you feel breath at your back. Not threatening, not urgent. Simply present. A reminder that something unfinished walks with you.

You keep a careful watch. You avoid places where oaths are sworn recklessly. You refuse to witness vows made in anger or desperation. You learn to recognize when truth would shatter more than it would mend. This is the work of balance. Not heroic. Not clean. Necessary.

Years pass. The storm fades into legend—not forgotten, but diminished. Children hear stories of a time when the sky almost broke itself open. Druids argue quietly about what truly happened. Some insist the prophecy was restored. Others claim it was sealed. Both are wrong. It was contained. The relics you carried change with time. The Rune-Shard (Tara) grows inert, its hum silenced, its edges dulled. You keep it wrapped and hidden, bringing it out only when the air tightens, and the sky feels too aware. The Oath-Stone Fragment crumbles at last into grit, its purpose exhausted. You scatter it at a crossroads, where old words go to rest. The marks on your skin remain faint but visible. Those who know how to look can see them. Those who do not see nothing at all. That, too, is part of the balance.

In your later years, you return to Tara alone. The hill is quiet. Grass grows thick between the stones. The cracks remain, but they no longer glow. Kestrels circle overhead. Wind moves freely again. You sit beside the Lia Fáil, your back against cool stone. You think of what you did not say. You think of what might have been cleansed, renewed, remade. You also think of the villages that survived. The children who grew to adulthood under skies that did not burn. The kings who learned restraint. The storms that passed instead of lingering. Regret visits you. So does relief. As dusk settles, you feel the familiar pressure of the curse shift—not demanding, not growing—simply acknowledging the moment.

You speak softly to the stone, not prophecy, not confession. Only truth that harms no one. "I kept it together," you murmur. "I did what I could." The Lia Fáil remains silent. But the silence feels intentional. As night falls, the sky clears completely. Stars emerge one by one, sharp and cold and distant—no thunder rolls.

No pressure builds. The storm, such as it ever was, has learned to stay unfinished. You rise and leave the hill behind you. Your footsteps are steady. Your shadow follows at the proper distance. And Ériu remains—scarred, imperfect, alive.

# Chapter 26
## Ascension of the Stormwarden

THE SKY LOWERS TO meet you, not in threat, not in fury, but in recognition. Clouds spiral inward with deliberate grace, their vast arms curving around the Hill of Tara as though drawing a circle older than stone. Wind falls quiet. The air becomes charged and lucid, each breath sharp with ozone and clarity. Above, lightning does not strike; it writes, etching pale sigils across the underbellies of clouds, repeating the language you learned when you let the storm inside your bones.

You stand at the hill's crown, where the stones remember kings and judges and liars alike. The Lia Fáil glows—not with fracture-light now, but with a steady radiance that seems to rise from deep within the earth. Its crack has widened just enough to admit a truth long denied. You feel no fear. The Storm-Sigil no longer hums as an object. It is a rhythm in your blood. The Ancestral Thread no longer pulls. It has braided itself into you, binding mortal marrow to divine cadence. Where once the storm circled and tested, now it listens. The Ancestral Chorus gathers—not whispering, not admonishing, but singing. Their voices layer and lift, forming a harmony that steadies the air and holds the clouds in place. It is time, they sing. Not to mend. To name.

You step into the ring of stones. Mist peels back—grass bows. The standing stones turn, not physically, but in meaning, their runes aligning, their fractures brightening like veins carrying fire rather than lightning. The hill has accepted you as more than a witness. You lift your hands. Lightning arcs between your palms, thin and precise, a filament rather than a bolt. It does not burn. It listens. You shape it with thought and breath, guiding its tension, easing its hunger. This is not the wild lightning of terror and chance. This is the storm taught to kneel.

Above you, the godborn storm descends. It does not crash. It does not roar. It approaches. The vast humanoid shape takes form within the clouds—limbs of wind, a crown of rotating lightning, a face that flickers no longer. It steadies into something singular and solemn, no longer divided by stolen truths or buried prophecy. It lowers itself until its presence fills the sky above Tara, immense and contained. "You have finished me," it says—not aloud, but in the deep places of your chest where breath and will meet. "You have given me shape."

You meet its gaze without flinching. "I have named you," you reply. Your voice carries—not because you shout, but because the storm recognizes authority when it hears it. "And I will not be ruled by what I create." A pause stretches—vast, delicate. Then the storm kneels. Wind presses outward in a wide, gentle ring. The grass flattens, not crushed but honored. The stones vibrate, their runes singing in response. Far across Ériu, thunder rolls—not in warning, but in acknowledgment. The godborn storm bows its crowned head. "Then take the charge," it says. "Be the hand that guides my force. Be the boundary I could not be."

The sky opens, not with rain, but with light. A column descends, white-blue and pure, enveloping you in a brilliance that does not blind. You feel your body lighten, not dissolving, but refining. Pain flashes once—brief, clarifying—as mortal limits loosen their grip. You remember everything. Your first breath. The bog's cold pull. The moment you chose control over fear. The truth you spoke and the truths you bent. You feel no regret—only alignment. The land accepts you.

Power settles into you—not explosive, not intoxicating, but vast and steady. You feel the pressure systems of the sky like tides in your veins. You feel the fault-lines of truth beneath stone. You feel the places where storms will form—and the places where they must not. You are no longer merely in the world. You are with it. The transformation completes without spectacle. The light withdraws. The storm remains kneeling. You stand, unchanged to mortal eyes, same face, same hands, but the air around you has altered. It listens differently. It waits. The Lia Fáil answers at last. A low, resonant sound rises from the stone—not a cry for a king, but a tone of recognition deeper and older than crowns. The hill has found its warden.

Across Ériu, the effects ripple outward. Storms still come, but they break cleanly and move on. Rivers swell but do not drown their banks—lightning strikes where it must—fire-clearing, boundary-marking, never wanton. The land breathes easier under a sky that has learned restraint. Kings feel it. Some grow cautious. Some grow resentful. None can deny it. They no longer rule alone. You do not take a throne. You do not wear a crown. You establish no law written in blood or ink. Instead, you become a presence, appearing where storms gather too tightly, where truth begins to sharpen into weapons. You speak rarely. When you do, the sky stills.

Temples rise to you without your command, circles of stone open to the air, where offerings are left not in fear but in respect. You accept none that seek to bind you. You accept those given freely, then disperse them, rain for fields, wind for sails, silence for grief. The relics you once carried are no longer objects. The Rune-Shard (Tara) dissolves into the stones, its work complete. The Storm-Sigil becomes the cadence of your breath. The Ancestral Thread quiets, its purpose fulfilled in continuity rather than claim. Mortality loosens its hold.

You still walk among people, but years pass without touching you. Faces you knew age and fade. Children grow and bring their own children to stand on the hill and point upward when thunder rolls gently, saying, "The Stormwarden is watching." You are not worshiped as a god of conquest or demand. You are named in the old way. Warden. Balancer. The One Who Stands When the Sky Bends.

Once, long after the last stone cracked and healed, you stand alone on Tara at dusk. The sky is clear. Stars prick the dark like seeds waiting for rain. You consider what you surrendered. A simple life. A mortal ending. The ease of not knowing. You consider what you gained. A land that endures. A storm that kneels. A prophecy finished without being weaponized. The wind brushes your face, gentle and knowing. Above, clouds gather far away, where they should. You turn your gaze outward and lift one hand. The storm obeys.

# Chapter 27
# The Tragic Stand

YOU DO NOT RUN. The storm expects that. It has learned the shapes of fear—flight, pleading, surrender. It has felt mortals break themselves open to survive beneath its pressure. You deny it that satisfaction. The sky has split into motion above you, clouds tearing and reforming in violent spirals. Wind lashes the land flat. Lightning strikes without rhythm now, jagged and furious, cracking the hillsides and setting fire to hedges already stripped bare by rain. This is no longer a storm seeking completion. This is a storm enraged by refusal.

You stand at the ancient convergence ground—an old place where storms once died rather than spread. The stones here are shattered remnants, half-buried, scorched black by lightning long forgotten. Druids once believed this place could unmake a storm by grounding its fury into earth and bone. They were wrong—the ground trembles beneath your boots. Thunder slams down in continuous waves, rattling your ribs, making your teeth ache. Each breath tastes of ash and ozone.

The storm descends, not kneeling, not shaping itself carefully, but crashing down-ward like a god throwing itself against the world. Its vast form fills the sky: limbs of wind, a face fractured into many ex-pressions—rage, hunger, wounded pride. Lightning pours from it like blood from an open wound. "YOU COULD HAVE GUIDED ME." The voice tears through you, splitting thought from thought. "YOU COULD HAVE GIVEN ME FORM."

You plant your feet. "I will not become your vessel," you shout back, voice almost lost in the gale. "And I will not kneel to what feeds on fracture." The storm laughs—a sound like mountains grinding together. "THEN YOU WILL BE REMEMBERED AS RE-SISTANCE."

You draw the last of what you carry—not relic, not rune, but will. The old rites come back to you, not as clean incantations but as instincts carved into bone by long-dead teachers. You cut your palm with a shard of stone. Blood falls to the ground, hissing as lightning strikes nearby. The earth answers faintly, but it is already overwhelmed. The convergence ground shudders, its ancient protections straining like rotted ropes. You raise your bleeding hand to the sky. "Here," you say. "Take this instead." You open yourself—not to communion, not to surrender—but to defiance. You anchor yourself as deeply as you can, forcing your presence downward into soil and stone, becoming a living conduit meant to ground the storm's fury.

The pain is immediate and unbearable. Lightning slams into you—not a single strike, but a continuous torrent. Your vision whites out. Your body arches, every nerve screaming as the storm pours through you, seeking release. For one brief, terrible moment, it works. The storm stutters. Its pressure collapses inward, thunder faltering mid-roar. The wind drops sharply, as if the world has gasped.

Far across Ériu, clouds tear apart. Rivers stop rising. Fires gutter. You feel the storm hesitate. Then it realizes what you are doing. "YOU ARE TOO SMALL," it snarls—not cruelly, but almost regretfully. "YOU ARE NOT MEANT TO HOLD THIS."

Your knees buckle. You fall to one side, catching yourself on a broken stone slick with rain. Blood runs freely now, mixing with water, soaking into earth already overburdened by power. The convergence ground begins to crack. Lightning strikes the stones directly, shattering what remains of their ancient structure. The last protections fail. The storm surges again—stronger, angrier, no longer restrained by hesitation. You feel something tear inside you. Not flesh. Identity. Your memories begin to slip, not vanish, but fragment. Names loosen. Faces blur. The storm is burning through the places where self is held, consuming resistance as fuel.

You scream, not in pain, but in fury. "No," you snarl through clenched teeth. "Not like this." You force yourself upright one last time. The storm looms directly overhead now, immense and unstoppable. Lightning coils around you like chains. Your shadow flickers wildly across the shattered stones. You know, finally, clearly, that this is the end. Not of the land. Of you. And so you choose the only victory left. You release the anchor. You let go of control, not to submit, but to misdirect.

With the last of your strength, you twist your stance, turning your body away from the land and toward the sky, redirecting the storm's surge upward instead of downward. Lightning tears through you in a final, blinding arc. The storm screams—not in triumph, but in shock—as its force is hurled skyward, scattered, thinned, robbed of cohesion. The clouds rip apart. Thunder breaks into disordered echoes. Rain falls suddenly, hard, cleansing, uncontrolled. You fall.

When the storm finally passes, it does so in pieces. No single towering presence remains. No godborn shape stalks the sky. Instead, weather returns to what it once was: dangerous, unpredictable, but not sentient. Not hunting. Ériu survives. Bare-ly. The convergence ground is a ruin. The ancient stones are gone entirely, reduced to splintered black shards fused into the earth. The hillside smolders where lightning struck repeatedly, grass burned away to reveal raw soil beneath. At the center lies a body. Yours.

Those who find you days later—druids, villagers, shepherds drawn by rumor and fear—do not recognize you at first. The marks on your skin are burned away. Your face is calm, strangely intact, as though the storm took everything else instead. They bury you where you fell. No cairn marks the spot. No stone dares stand upright there again. The land around it grows back slowly, cautiously, as if remembering pain. Stories spread.

Some say you challenged the storm and lost. Others say you broke it at the cost of yourself. Children are warned not to go near the place where lightning strikes without thunder. Druids speak your name softly during rites of protection, not as a god, but as a boundary. The storm never fully returns to Ériu. Weather remains fierce, but it never gathers with intention again. Never again does it listen. And sometimes—only sometimes—when lightning flashes far away, those who are sensitive swear they hear a voice beneath the thunder. Not commanding. Not pleading. Laughing, faint and defiant. As if something mortal once stood against the sky and did not yield.

# Chapter 28
# The Storm's Release

YOU DO NOT HESITATE. Hesitation is how things break without meaning. You stand at the center of the ritual ground, lightning locked in rigid arcs above you, sigils blazing with a light that hurts to look at, and you finally understand what the storm has been asking for all along. Not obedience. Not worship. Not even freedom. Release.

Your hands rise—not in command, not in surrender, but in farewell. You drive the blade down into the first sigil. The sound is not thunder. It is deeper, older—a tearing noise like the sky itself being ripped open along a seam it never meant to expose. The sigil fractures instantly, light spraying outward in shards that burn the air where they strike. The pressure inside your skull spikes so violently you scream, the sound torn from you and scattered by the wind. The storm surges.

You cut the second sigil before it can stop you. Pain flares white-hot, raw and blinding, as the binding loosens unevenly. Lightning crashes downward, no longer frozen, slamming into stone with explosive force. The ritual circle buckles, great slabs of scorched earth tearing free and lifting into the air as if gravity has forgotten its purpose. The storm roars—not in triumph, not in fury, but in motion.

You carve the third sigil apart with hands slick with blood and rain that has finally begun to fall. The sky convulses, clouds tearing themselves open as the compressed force uncoils in a violent cascade. Wind screams across the plain, flattening grass, ripping stones loose, scouring the land clean.

Druin is far away now—too far to reach, too far to matter. You catch one last glimpse of him braced against a standing stone, cloak snapping wildly, eyes wide not with fear, but understanding. He knows what you have chosen.

You tear apart the final sigil. The binding collapses. The storm erupts. Lightning detonates outward in a blinding web, no longer confined to a single sky but racing across Ériu in a roaring front of light and sound. Thunder follows not as a single voice, but as a thousand overlapping crashes that shake the bones of the world. Rain slams down in sheets so heavy they blur the land into shadow and motion. You are thrown backward. Stone smashes against your ribs. Breath leaves your body in a violent rush. The world spins, sky and ground exchanging places in flashes of white and black. For a moment—just a moment—you think you have died.

Then pain returns. You are alive. Barely. The storm does not linger. Freed from compression, it moves the way storms were always meant to move—violent, devastating, finite. It tears across the land in a single, unstoppable surge, breaking where it must, cleansing what it touches without discrimination. Trees fall. Rivers flood. Cliffs shear away into roaring seas. Villages suffer. Some are lost. Some are scarred. Some are spared by chance alone. The destruction is terrible—but it does not repeat. It does not circle back. It does not wait hungrily for another victim.

It passes. And when it does, the sky empties. Clouds thin into ragged remnants. Lightning fades into memory. Thunder retreats beyond the horizon, carrying the last echoes of the godborn force with it. Silence follows. Not the suffocating silence of containment—but the exhausted quiet that comes after something immense has spent itself.

You lie amid shattered stone and soaked earth, lungs burning, vision blurred. Rain washes blood from your hands. Your body feels wrong—too light in places, too heavy in others—but it is yours again. The pressure that once filled your skull is gone. The storm is no longer inside you. Nor above you. It is simply… weather again. Days pass before you can stand without swaying.

Druin returns with others—druids, villagers, survivors carrying the stunned expressions of people who have lived through something they will never fully explain. They do not cheer you. They do not kneel. They help you walk. Ériu bears the scars openly. Fields are torn apart. Coastlines reshaped. Forests flattened into tangled ruin. But beneath the devastation, something stirs that had long been suppressed. The land breathes differently now—no longer compressed by trapped divinity, no longer strained by forced control.

New growth comes quickly in unexpected places. Green shoots push through ash-blackened soil. Rivers settle into new courses, carving fertile banks where none existed before. The storm, in its final fury, has stripped away rot as well as life. The prophecy does not return. There is no final verse declaring salvation or doom. The fragments fade, their work done—not fulfilled, but spent. You understand now that some prophecies are not meant to be completed. They exist only to force a choice.

You walk Ériu as a living reminder of that choice. People tell stories of you—contradictory, half-true, shaped by fear and gratitude in equal measure. Some call you Stormbreaker. Others call you Ruin-Bringer. Children grow up hearing that once, long ago, someone stood against the sky and survived. Kings still rule in some places. Councils rise in others. No divine voice crowns them. No storm waits hungrily above their halls. Law and failure belong entirely to mortal hands again.

And you— You age. Slowly, painfully, honestly. Your scars never fully fade. When storms roll in, you feel them before clouds appear, a faint ache in old bones, a memory of pressure long released. But the storms pass, and you let them.

On your final return to Tara, the hill stands quiet beneath an open sky. The Lia Fáil remains cracked, its silver seam dull and inert. Ravens perch on stone and take flight when you approach, unafraid. You kneel—not to pray, not to command—but to rest your hand on weathered rock. The land does not speak. It does not need to. The storm is gone. The world remains. And that, you realize at last, was always enough.

This is the ending you chose. Not dominion. Not destiny. But release. And Ériu endures—scarred, renewed, and free beneath a sky that no longer waits to be bound.

# Chapter 29
# Crown of Ruin

THE STORM DOES NOT ask again. It has learned your shape—your pauses, your silences, the places where truth thins and breaks. It has tasted the withheld word and found it nourishing. Where others fed it fear or defiance, you fed it control without confession, and that is a rarer thing. The Hill of Tara lies beneath a sky that no longer pretends to be natural.

Clouds coil inward in disciplined spirals, layered and precise, as if stacked by an unseen hand. Lightning does not strike randomly. It marks boundaries. It traces lines from stone to stone, etching a map only you can read. The air hums with restrained violence, held taut like a drawn bow that never releases. You stand within the ring. The Lia Fáil is no longer merely cracked. Its fissure yawns wide, glowing with a cold, imperial light. The stone has not broken—it has opened. What was buried beneath prophecy and fear now breathes freely.

You feel the curse settle fully into you. No longer a whisper. No longer a damp pressure on your back. It has found its seat—behind your eyes, beneath your tongue, in the hollow where unspoken truths gather and rot. You do not flinch. You have learned what others have not: silence can be sharper than confession. Control can be cleaner than redemption.

Above you, the godborn storm descends. Not kneeling, approaching as an equal. Its vast form gathers shape—wind and lightning disciplined into something unmistakably regal. The face that forms within the clouds no longer flickers between possibilities. It steadies, mirroring the restraint you taught it. "You did not finish me," the storm says, voice smooth as polished stone. "You refined me." You lift your gaze. "I did what was necessary," you reply. Your voice carries effortlessly. The wind bends to it. "Truth breaks the world when spoken without measure." The storm's lightning crown tightens, condensing into a single arc that circles its brow. "And you measured well."

The Ancestral Chorus does not gather. They are silent. You feel them recoil into stone and soil, withdrawing from a future they no longer recognize. The hill accepts their retreat. The land has learned to endure worse. You step forward. The storm lowers—not in submission, but in alignment. Pressure equalizes between sky and flesh. You feel no transformation like the ascension offered before. This is not apotheosis. This is enthronement.

The Rune-Shard (Tara) rises unbidden from your pouch, its edges sharp once more. It splits in your grasp—not fracturing, but unfolding—its pieces locking together into a circlet of carved light that hovers just above your brow. A crown. Not of gold. Not of stone. Of unfinished prophecy. You do not hesitate. You let it settle. The moment it touches you, the storm exhales. Across Ériu, thunder rolls—not as warning, not as cleansing rain, but as declaration. Lightning strikes in perfect symmetry along ridges and coasts, branding the land with your presence. You feel everything.

Pressure systems are shifting continents away. Rivers are tightening their courses. Winds are adjusting their long-held routes. The storm no longer assembles itself in hunger or confusion. It assembles when you permit it. You turn slowly, surveying the hill. The standing stones bow—not physically, but in meaning. Their runes dim, then reconfigure, aligning themselves beneath your authority. The Lia Fáil emits a deep, resonant tone—not recognition, not welcome. Submission. You are no longer bound by what the stone once demanded of kings. You are what it feared. You raise one hand.

The storm responds instantly, coiling tighter, darker, heavier. Clouds descend until they brush the hilltop, misting your cloak with cold rain that evaporates before it reaches the ground. Villages below fall silent. Animals flee or kneel. Druids feel it first—the severing. The old channels of communion go quiet. Prayers fall upward and do not return. Sacred groves wither where storms once whispered guidance. You have not destroyed the gods. You have outpaced them. Kings gather armies. They do not march. Each attempt to raise banners is answered by measured catastrophe. Floods that stop short of total ruin, lightning that strikes storehouses but spares homes. Enough loss to teach obedience. Not enough to invite rebellion.

You rule without a throne. Without law. Without mercy. And without chaos. The storm is your instrument, precise and devastating. You deploy it sparingly, surgically. You allow seasons to proceed. Crops grow under skies that never fully clear. Fear becomes routine. Routine becomes order. Children are taught to watch the clouds for signs, not of weather, but of your attention. Your silence becomes doctrine. Speak too much, and storms follow. Speak carefully, and survive.

Over time, stories shift. They no longer speak of the Seer who stood between stone and sky. They speak of the Storm-King. The Crowned Silence. The One Who Holds Thunder in Their Mouth. Your shadow no longer behaves as shadows should. It stretches long and deep, pooling at your feet even under full sun. Within it, faint shapes move—echoes of the bog's curse, now disciplined, now weaponized. The mouth within the shadow never opens. It does not need to.

Years pass. You do not age. Your presence stabilizes the storm permanently, but at a terrible cost. Without uncertainty, without chance, the land hardens. Innovation slows. Joy thins. Survival becomes exacting, joyless, obedient. Ériu does not collapse. It calcifies. The storm kneels to no one but you. And you kneel to nothing at all.

On the final page of prophecy, unwritten, unspoken, but felt in every breath, the truth becomes clear: You did not fail to stop the storm. You became what it was meant to crown. At last, alone upon Tara under a sky that never fully clears, you feel a flicker of something unfamiliar. Not regret. Not fear. A distant curiosity. You look upward, into the disciplined spiral of clouds, and wonder—not whether you were right but whether anything will ever be able to undo you. The storm does not answer. It waits.

# Chapter 30
# Wild Renewal

YOU DO NOT CROWN anyone. You do not carve a new law into stone. You do not gather the broken pieces of kingship and try to bind them into a shape the land might tolerate. You stand on Tara's wind-cut crown and feel the old hunger for order—the mortal desire to set a hand upon chaos and call it finished—and you let that hunger pass through you like cold rain. The land has been commanded for too long. So you step back. Not as surrender. As refusal.

Below, Ériu is loud with uncertainty. Without kings, the world does not become gentle. It becomes honest. The first days after the fall of crowns are not sung about in the way bards prefer. They are messy, frightened, sharpened by hunger and old grudges that no longer fear a king's punishment. Men who once bowed to banners now bow only to necessity. Families pack what they can carry and move toward kin. Warriors without warbands look for purpose like starving dogs sniffing smoke.

And still—beneath the fear—the land exhales. Fields that had turned stubborn under false rule do not become generous overnight. But they begin to answer again when tended with care, not tribute. Rivers run where they will, no longer redirected for the pride of halls. The Lia Fáil remains cracked, yet its hum steadies, like a wound that will not close but has stopped bleeding.

You feel the change in small, unglorious ways. A village that once sent half its grain to a distant hall keeps enough to feed its children through winter. A widow who would have been ignored by law is listened to at a hearth-circle because she remembers the old boundary-stones and can name where the water once ran. A young hunter, quick with jokes and quicker with aim, is chosen to lead not because his father held a title, but because he returns from the woods with meat and does not hoard it. No one calls it a new age.

They simply begin living differently, because they must.

The first councils are awkward. People gather in circles out of habit—because the shape feels older than thrones. Someone speaks too loudly and is mocked. Someone speaks too softly and is ignored—arguments last until dawn. Decisions are made, reversed, made again. In some places, hot tempers win and blood answers. In others, elders pull the young aside and remind them that a village is not a battlefield, and that the land does not feed those who burn their own roof for spite.

There are failures. There are betrayals. There are days when you hear news of violence, and you taste the old urge to intervene—to step forward and make your voice into law. But you do not. Because you know what that becomes.

You travel, not as ruler and not as savior, but as witness and warning. You carry no crown. You carry no sacred code. You carry only what Tara has left you: an understanding that truth cannot be commanded into goodness, only allowed to reshape what is rotten.

Where you arrive, people ask you to decide for them. They do it with fear first, then with reverence. Some fall to their knees as though you have become the land's new mouth. Some glare, seeing in you the one who shattered their certainty and left them to stand unguarded. "Tell us what to do," they say. "Name who should lead." "Bind us together again."

You answer the same way each time. "I will not choose for you," you tell them. "If you hand your will to another, you will one day find your hands empty." Some curse you for it. Some listen. And some—quiet, stubborn—begin to understand what you are really giving them: the burden and the blessing of shaping their own world.

As seasons turn, patterns form. Not one pattern. Many. In the western hills, clans return to older customs, electing leaders each year by acclaim and deed. In the fertile lowlands, villages form alliances, sharing grain and defense, bound by mutual oaths spoken in the open air where the land can hear. Along the coasts, fisherfolk create councils that rotate responsibilities, refusing any permanent voice that might become a fist.

In some places, warlords rise, trying to seize the old shape of kingship by force. The land does not bless them. But men do not always require a blessing to kill. There are skirmishes, raids, and brutal winters. Some communities fail and scatter. Some leaders grow cruel. Some councils become tyrannies in all but name, hiding power behind collective speech.

And yet, the difference endures: When rule turns rotten, it can be torn out like a weed. There is no divine crown to protect it. No inherited right to make it sacred. People who have tasted choice do not return easily to chains.

You witness this in a valley where a self-made lord tries to demand tribute and obedience. He rides with armed men and calls himself protector. He speaks the language of the old halls, expecting it to work still. The villagers listen. Then an old woman steps forward, hands stained with earth, and says, "We have protected our-selves for generations. You did not ask the land. You asked only your own hunger." Others join her—not shouting, not kneel-ing, simply standing, refusing.

The would-be lord's men hesitate. Some-thing in the air changes. Not magic, not thunder—only the quiet realization that power is not a thing that can be taken once and kept forever. It must be fed. And a people who will not feed it can starve it into nothing. The lord leaves. Not because you intervened. Because the valley chose itself.

At Tara, the stones remain scarred. They do not mend into the old circle. They do not pretend the fracture never happened. The Lia Fáil's crack stays visible, a silver seam through weathered stone. Ravens still perch there at dawn, silent, watchful, as though guarding the memory of what once was.

Pilgrims come sometimes. Not to crown kings, but to speak vows with the hill lis-tening. To confess. To ask forgiveness from soil rather than from thrones. To leave of-ferings of salt and oat and iron, small signs of respect to a land that has outlasted every ruler who tried to claim it.

The storm does not vanish from the world. But it changes. It no longer gathers into a single godborn hunger seeking a doorway. The old focal point—your blood, Tara's fracture, Maelchon's lie—has been dispersed into something broader and less personal. Storms come as storms should: harsh, sometimes deadly, but no longer intent. No longer stalking a crown-shaped absence in the world.

And you— You feel yourself slowly returning to the scale of a person. Not fully. Never fully. Tara has marked you, and once marked, no one is simply mortal again. You carry the memory of law beneath stone and the weight of what you refused to become. Sometimes, on quiet nights, you still hear the faintest murmur of the Ancestral Chorus like wind in old reeds—not commanding, not pleading. Remember, it seems to say. Do not let them forget.

So you do what you can. You teach oaths to be spoken plainly and kept with care. You warn against men who crave permanence. You remind councils that mercy is not weakness, and that the land remembers cruelty long after banners have rotted. You walk the roads between communities that rise, fail, and rise again.

You watch children who were born after kings fell grow into adults who cannot imagine bending their necks for a crown. You see new songs take shape—songs that do not praise a ruler's bloodline, but a village that endured a winter together, a council that admitted its wrong and changed, a leader who stepped down when their time passed. It is not peace. It is not tidy. It is not a story that ends cleanly with triumph and a kneeling storm. It is a living, breathing world learning how to hold itself. Ériu becomes wilder. And, slowly—unevenly, honestly—it becomes free.

When you return to Tara at last, years later or only months, time feels strange once you have heard the land's oldest voice—you stand among the broken stones and feel the hill's steady hum beneath your feet. No crown rests here. No throne claims the sky. Only stone. Mist. Memory. Choice.

And as dawn bleeds pale gold through thinning cloud, you understand the ending you have chosen: Not a single destiny fulfilled— But a thousand destinies allowed to begin. The land does not belong to one voice. It belongs to those who listen.

# Chapter 31
## The Age of Hands and Minds

NO OMEN MARKS THE turning. No raven circles a shrine. No standing stone cracks open to spill a final warning. The sky offers only weather—clouds gathering, breaking, passing on—indifferent to the lives beneath. If the gods ever leaned close enough to be heard, they do not now. Their silence does not arrive like punishment. It comes like an unlocked door left swinging in the wind, and one day, people simply stop waiting for someone to close it. They begin, instead, to build.

At first, it is small, almost accidental. A healer in a river village notices that boiling water keeps fever from spreading through a household. A midwife marks the difference between clean cloth and dirty. A farmer writes down which fields recover after a flood and which remain sickly, and teaches a neighbor how to read the notes.

None of it feels sacred. It feels practical. It feels humble. It works.

Word travels faster than prayer. Those who once would have walked to shrines with offerings now walk to those who have learned something useful. A few old priests object, calling it arrogance. Most are simply relieved. Relief is a quiet thing, but it spreads like sunlight in a long winter.

The first true houses of healing do not call themselves temples. They are built beside wells and crossroads, where travelers can be seen, counted, and tended. Herbs are stored not as charms but as medicine. Wounds are cleaned. Fever is isolated. Loss still comes—no age ends death—but death's face changes. It becomes less mysterious, less triumphant. Less easily blamed on curses and offended spirits. People begin to ask different questions. Not: What did we do to deserve this? But: What can we do to prevent it?

The old stories do not vanish. They soften. Children still hear of Manannán's mist and the Sidhe's hollow hills, of storms that wore faces and heroes who bargained with the sky. But the stories shift from instruction to metaphor. The godborn storm becomes a warning about pride. The cracked stones of Tara become a reminder that power breaks when hoarded. Myth turns inward, a mirror rather than a map.

And the world grows wider. Trade expands not because kings demand tribute, but because roads are safer when communities maintain them together. Ports grow into cities where languages mingle. Tools improve. Navigation sharpens. Merchants begin to carry more than goods: they carry methods, remedies, ideas, and arguments. Arguments become the new prophecy—loud, imperfect, necessary.

In councils and markets, people debate what once would have been declared by druids. How should land be shared? Who should lead? What is owed to those who suffer? No divine voice ends the conversation. That means the conversation does not end cleanly. It also means it belongs to everyone brave enough to speak. Some kings resist. They long for the old world, where a crown could claim legitimacy by pointing to a blessing no one could question. But blessings no longer arrive. The stones do not cry out. The skies do not validate. Authority must become negotiated rather than inherited. Some crowns fall. Others transform—becoming less like sacred symbols and more like responsibilities weighed by those who are governed.

This is not a gentle age. There are still wars. There are still famines. There are still years when rain comes wrong, and whole villages must move or starve. But the response changes. Neighboring regions send grain not as charity bestowed by a ruler, but as investment in shared survival. Healers travel. Knowledge is exchanged. People begin to understand that suffering in one corner of the land does not remain politely contained.

Global support—though they do not call it global yet—takes root in the simplest recognition. We are not separate enough to be safe alone. When plague threatens one coast, ships are halted, not by superstition, but by containment. When floods carve a valley open, engineers—men and women who would once have been priests of water—arrive with tools and plans. When a harsh winter kills cattle, herds are redistributed so that no single clan collapses entirely. The old tribal grudges remain, but they are increasingly outweighed by the blunt arithmetic of survival.

And slowly, something rare happens. The world learns to encourage itself. Songs are written not only of heroes, but of communities rebuilding. The bards sing of healers who stood through night watches, of builders who raised walls against storm, of council leaders who chose compromise over bloodshed. There is glory, yes—but it is found in endurance and service rather than divine favor. A great library is built where a shrine once stood. Its roof is plain, sturdy. Its walls are lined with written knowledge: remedies, observations, debates, maps. Visitors arrive with questions and leave with more questions, which is considered progress rather than doubt. Children learn to read not so they can recite prayers properly, but so they can understand what others have learned before them.

The last druids become scholars. Some mourn what has been lost—the old hum of stones, the feeling of being listened to by sky and spirit. Others admit, quietly, that divine attention was never as merciful as the stories claimed. The gods did not prevent suffering. Prophecy did not stop tyrants. Magic was powerful, yes—but it was never evenly distributed, never reliably kind.

Now the world must carry its own burden. And it does. Not always well. Not always nobly. But deliberately. You are remembered only in fragments in this age—if you are remembered at all. A footnote in an old chronicle mentions a Seer who cut the Thread and "ended the whispering between blood and sky." Some interpret it as sacrilege. Some interpret it as liberation. Most do not care. The age has moved on. People have more urgent concerns than the identity of a long-dead figure.

Still, your choice lingers like a foundation stone beneath their feet. Because it is not only magic that fades, it is excuse. No longer can a ruler say, "The gods demanded it." No longer can a priest say, "Fate decreed it." No longer can a clan say, "The land chose us." People must own their decisions fully. That ownership is heavy. It is also clarifying.

In time, nations—many, varied, frequently quarrelsome—begin forming treaties not sealed by sacred oath, but by mutual benefit. They share knowledge of medicine. They establish systems for responding to disasters. They start exchanging healers and builders across borders. Trust is fragile, but it grows where it is rewarded. Betrayal still happens, but it is answered by consequence rather than cosmic mystery. War does not vanish. But it becomes harder to justify. When death is no longer wrapped in myth, its cost becomes more visible. When disasters are understood rather than feared as divine will, people see that suffering is not inevitable—it is often preventable. Those who seek power through cruelty find themselves facing not a storm's wrath, but the united refusal of those who have learned to rebuild together.

There comes a year, later spoken of as The Great Outpouring. A fever sweeps across regions too vast to be contained by any single ruler's decree. In another age, it would have been called a curse. In this one, it is studied. Isolated. Countered. People travel carrying not swords but supplies. Healers share methods freely. Cities open stores of grain to feed those who cannot work. Villages shelter strangers. Many die. But not as many as would have. And afterward, there is a strange thing in the air—not divine blessing, not omen—but a collective understanding: we saved each other.

That knowledge becomes sacred. Not the kind that demands worship, but the type that demands responsibility. In your final pages, the world does not become perfect. It does not become gentle. It does not transcend human flaws. It merely becomes human in full, no longer leaning on invisible forces to justify its worst instincts or its finest hopes. Ériu endures beneath a sky that offers no prophecy.

And yet, there is wonder. Not in runes glowing beneath stone, but in hands learning to mend. In minds refusing ignorance. In communities choosing to build rather than burn. In the quiet courage of people who accept that the world will not be saved by gods—and decide to save it anyway, as best they can.

There is a last scene, told in a story that has no reason to remember you, and yet somehow does. An old person sits beside a child on a hill where stones once stood sacred. The child points to the clouds and asks what they mean. The elder considers the question and smiles—not sadly, but with calm certainty. "They mean rain, sometimes," the elder says. "They mean wind, sometimes. They mean we should bring the animals in, or that we will need water for the crops." "And do they ever mean something else?" the child asks. The elder looks at the wide land below—fields, roads, houses, people moving like living threads across the earth. "They mean," the elder says, "that we must pay attention." Not to gods. To each other.

# Chapter 32
## Tyranny of Sacred Law

YOU DO NOT REACH for a crown. Crowns can be removed. You reach instead for permanence. The place where you carve the new law is not a hall and not a hilltop, but a convergence of stone and soil where the old authority once spoke most clearly—where the land still listens even after centuries of silence. You choose it deliberately, knowing that whatever is set here will echo outward until there is no corner of Ériu untouched by its weight.

You kneel. You cut. You bind. The sacred law does not bloom the way the old one did. It does not hum with memory or breathe with patience. It locks. You inscribe it with words that do not bend: conditions, prohibitions, consequences. You remove ambiguity. You strip mercy from places where it once softened judgment. Where the land once listened, it now enforces. Where people once argued, the stone now answers for them. And the land accepts it. Not gladly. Not gently. But completely.

The soil stiffens beneath your hands as if learning a new posture. Standing stones across Ériu are quiet, their cracks dimming as though sealed by unseen mortar. Rivers hold to their banks with unnatural obedience. Storms lose their wandering nature, breaking only where the law allows them to break. Chaos retreats.

Violence falters mid-breath, as though struck by sudden certainty. Feuds unravel when the law names an outcome before blades are drawn. Warlords find their voices failing when they speak commands not aligned with the binding code. Councils still gather—but their debates shorten, choices narrowing until only one path remains.

Stability returns with alarming speed. Fires burn evenly. Crops grow in disciplined rows. Roads are repaired and remain repaired. Theft dwindles, not because hunger has vanished, but because punishment arrives with mechanical precision. Children grow up knowing exactly what is expected of them—and exactly what will happen if they fail.

At first, the people are grateful. They are tired of fear. Tired of choosing. Tired of living with the raw consequences of freedom. They praise the calm. They praise the quiet. They praise you, though you never asked them to. They do not call you king. They call you Architect. Lawbearer. The One Who Ended the Breaking. You do not correct them. Because correction would require uncertainty, and uncertainty no longer exists as it once did.

Druin stands with you when the first edict takes effect. You feel him before you see him—his unease registering like a flaw in otherwise perfect stone. He has aged in the weeks since the law was set, lines cutting deeper around his eyes, his posture careful, as though the ground itself might object if he stands too freely. "It holds," he says, watching a distant village where a long-standing feud dissolves without bloodshed. "Too well." "The land needed structure," you reply. Your voice carries further than it used to, steady and un-moved by the wind. "It was tearing itself apart." Druin nods slowly. "Yes. But you have given it a spine that cannot bend."

You turn to him. For a moment—just a moment—you consider loosening some-thing and allowing an exception. A mercy clause. A space where judgment can soften when circumstances demand it. The law does not allow it. Not because it forbids you—but because you understand, now, that allowing mercy would introduce vari-ance. Variance would become interpreta-tion. Interpretation would become argu-ment. And argument would become frac-ture. You let the thought pass.

Druin sees the decision settle in you and flinches as though he has watched a door close forever. "You have made something that will outlast us all," he says quietly. "Yes," you answer. "That was the point."

He studies you then—not with accusa-tion, not with reverence, but with a kind of mourning reserved for things that cannot be unmade. "The land endures," he says.

"But people... they change. They will grow smaller under this." You do not deny it.

Over the years that follow, Ériu becomes orderly in ways it has never been. Crime becomes rare and predictable. Rebellion becomes almost impossible—not because of force, but because the law intercepts it before it gathers breath. Leadership exists, but only as a function, never as inspiration. Roles are assigned by precedent and statute, not by voice or vision.

Art thins. Songs still exist, but they praise outcomes rather than struggle. Stories teach obedience disguised as wisdom. Myths are preserved—but only as cautionary records of what chaos once looked like.

The land itself changes. Forests stop encroaching on settlements. Wildlife patterns stabilize into neat cycles. Even the storms seem disciplined, arriving on schedule, breaking cleanly, leaving minimal damage. The godborn tempest that once loomed as possibility never finds a doorway here. There is no space left for it.

And yet, beneath the calm, something dulls. You feel it most sharply when you walk among the people, and they step aside—not in fear, not in reverence, but in automatic compliance. Children do not ask you questions. Elders do not challenge you. Even Druin grows quieter with each passing season, his counsel shrinking to observation rather than warning.

One evening, long after the stones of Tara have cooled under starlight, he finally speaks what has been circling between you for years. "They no longer dream," he says. "Not dangerously. Not bravely." "They sleep safely," you reply. "Yes," Druin agrees. "And wake unchanged." He leaves soon after that. Not in exile. Not in rebellion. Simply gone—choosing a road that bends away from the centers of law, seeking whatever scraps of wildness remain beyond its reach. You do not stop him. The law does not require it.

As decades pass, you realize something unsettling: you are not aging the way others do. The sacred law has anchored you as profoundly as it has anchored Ériu. Time wears at you slowly, cautiously, as though unsure it has permission to proceed. You become a fixed point. A measure. A boundary.

People stop asking whether the law is just. They ask only whether it applies to them. When it does, they accept the outcome with resigned calm. When it does not, they adjust their behavior accordingly. There is no rebellion worth naming. There is no hero to rise against you. And that, perhaps, is the most complete victory of all.

Standing on Tara at night, you look out over a land that no longer trembles beneath its own weight. Fires burn evenly. Roads gleam pale in moonlight. The standing stones are silent, obedient, whole in a way they have never been before. The land has endured you.

But it no longer speaks. Not in whispers. Not in warnings. Not in possibility. You have given Ériu certainty—and in doing so, you have taken from it the dangerous gift of becoming something else.

Somewhere deep beneath stone and soil, the old law sleeps. Not dead. Not dreaming. Simply irrelevant. And you understand, finally, the cost of what you have built: A world without kings. A world without chaos. A world without mercy. A world that will never again need to choose. The storm never kneels here. It does not rage. It simply does not come.

You stand alone beneath a sky that obeys. And in that perfect, unyielding stillness, Ériu belongs—not to a crown, not to a people— but to the law you made eternal. This is the end you have chosen.

# Chapter 33
## The Last Blood Door

YOU DO NOT REACH for the storm as one reaches for a weapon. You open yourself the way earth opens to rain—without argument, without demand. The Ancestral Thread burns bright enough to ache behind your eyes, and for the first time, you understand that it has never been a leash or a crown. It has been a network—a lattice of inheritance stretched thin across generations, never meant to hold what it has been forced to carry. You step into what is awakening.

The storm does not kneel. It does not crown you. It recognizes. Pressure collapses inward, not violently, but decisively, like a breath finally released after centuries of restraint. Lightning slows. Thunder lowers its voice. The vast attention that once pressed upon the world narrows to a single, unbearable focus—you—and then begins to pass through you rather than into you.

The Ancestral Chorus falters. Not in protest. In completion. Names loosen from their song. Deeds unravel. The braided voices thin, one by one, until memory no longer arrives as instruction or warning, but as weather—present, shaping, impersonal. You feel yourself stretching across time rather than rising above it, your edges softening as the storm's force diffuses through your blood and beyond it.

Elsewhere, the change begins. It does not announce itself with omens. A young woman in the south—whose grandmother once dreamed of lightning—falls ill and does not recover. A child in the west, marked faintly by old rituals no one remembers clearly, is lost to a simple accident by the shore. An aging lord, long proud of a lineage he never fully understood, dies quietly in his sleep, his breath stopping as gently as a candle pinched out by familiar fingers. There is no pattern that can be mapped. No judgment that can be assigned. Only closure.

You feel each extinguishing not as pain, but as release—tiny knots loosening across a vast net. The storm's hunger diminishes with each passing, its need for vessels narrowing until it no longer reaches outward at all. The blood-doors are not sealed by decree. They simply fail to open. The world does not notice at first. Kings continue to rule. Children are born. Storms come and go with ordinary ferocity. There are no proclamations, no sudden hush in the sky. Only the slow disappearance of a danger most never knew existed.

You realize then what you have chosen. You are not becoming a god among many. You are becoming the last anchor. The storm does not collapse into you. It dissolves through you—into wind, into season, into the long mathematics of climate and pressure. You feel yourself thinning, dispersing, your sense of body loosening as if it were a garment no longer necessary to wear all at once. You are not everywhere. But you are distributed.

In the first winter after your choice, storms break cleanly along the coasts and pass inland without lingering. In the spring, rain comes late but steady, without omen or agenda. Lightning strikes where it always has—trees, ridges, open fields—never again seeking blood as a conduit. The sky has forgotten how to ask. You still exist, but existence feels different now. You do not walk the land as you once did. You experience it as movement, as change, as the slow turning of years that no longer pull at you personally. Your name fades first, then the shape of your face, then the idea that a single will ever stood at the center of so much consequence.

People tell fewer stories of Seers. Children grow up hearing storms described as dangers, not messages. Rituals lose their edge. Magic thins into symbolism—beautiful, harmless, unable to wound or save. The old stones remain, cracked and weathered, but no longer attentive. Moss claims their seams. Birds perch without hesitation.

You watch civilizations pass the way hills watch rivers—aware of motion, untouched by urgency. You see rulers rise who will never fear godborn catastrophe, who will never inherit power by accident of blood. Some govern well. Some do not. The difference no longer belongs to the sky. It belongs to people.

Immortality is not what you imagined. There is no throne, no endless vigilance, no worship to endure. There is only continuance. You are not prayed to because you cannot answer. You cannot intervene. You cannot decide. You are a principle now, not a presence—a final absorption of a mistake too large to be corrected any other way. Loneliness comes differently when time is no longer sharp. You miss small things: the weight of a body, the specificity of memory, the way names once mattered. But you do not regret the choice. Regret requires the belief that another ending would have been cleaner. There was no clean ending.

Centuries pass. The last traces of divine lineage disappear so thoroughly that scholars eventually argue whether such things ever truly existed. Storms are cataloged, studied, and measured. The sky becomes something humans map rather than fear. There are disasters—always—but none that arrive with intention. The prophecy dies quietly. Not shattered. Not fulfilled. Simply irrelevant.

You are there when it happens, though there is no moment to mark it. No final verse fades. No chorus mourns. The world continues without needing to remember why it is safer now. At some point—long after anyone might have expected—you stop thinking of yourself as "you." The storm does not return. It never will. It has already lived, already been born, already learned the shape of consequence. It has become the world's breath rather than its hunger. And you— You are the memory of a door that will never open again.

Ériu endures beneath a sky that no longer searches for blood, no longer tests worth, no longer waits for a vessel strong enough to bear it. The storm moves on. So does the world. And you remain—not as ruler, not as warning, but as the quiet certainty that some powers end not by force, but by being carried until there is nowhere left for them to go.

# Chapter 34
# The Living Cataclysm

YOU DO NOT CUT the sigils apart. You pull them in. The decision lands with a terrible calm, as if your body has been waiting for it longer than your mind ever dared to admit. You plant your feet at the center of the ritual ground, feel the stone's fractures biting cold through your soles, and draw a breath that scrapes your lungs raw. The storm presses. You answer.

You reach inward—not to memory, not to courage, but to the place where will becomes structure. You drag the binding across that threshold, carving it not with blade or chisel, but with intention so absolute it feels like violence turned inward. The first sigil tears free of the stone and sears itself into your skin. There is no scream. There is no mercy. Your flesh burns, then holds, the mark sinking beneath skin and muscle as if your body recognizes its purpose. Lightning recoils over-head, collapsing inward, drawn irresistibly toward the new anchor you have become.

The second sigil follows, ripping loose with a sound like tearing cloth soaked in rain. It does not settle on your body so much as into it, threading through nerve and bone, wrapping your spine in a lattice of pressure and restraint. Your vision fractures into white and black. You taste metal and ozone. Your heartbeat stutters, then synchronizes with something vast and terrible. The storm howls. Not in fury. In resistance. You pull harder.

The third sigil does not wait to be taken. It lunges, slamming into your chest with concussive force. You feel ribs crack—not break, but bend, reshaping to make room for containment never meant to be housed in flesh. The air screams as the storm collapses inward, its boundless motion forced into a singular point. Into you. The sky implodes.

Clouds spiral downward in violent compression, lightning folding back on itself in blinding arcs that vanish the instant they touch your skin. Thunder collapses into a deep, continuous pressure that vibrates through your bones rather than shaking the air. You fall to one knee. Then you rise again.

The storm is inside you now—not raging, not free, but contained, its endless motion arrested by a will it cannot circumvent. The sigils burn beneath your skin, brilliant lines of restraint etched through flesh, memory, and soul alike. Your breath slows. The land exhales. Across Ériu, the violence stops.

Storms that had gathered without release unravel into harmless rain. Winds lose their edge. The sky loosens its grip on the horizon. Rivers settle back into their beds, no longer surging with unnatural force. The pressure that had haunted coastlines and highlands alike dissipates as if a clenched fist has finally opened. The land stabilizes. You do not move. You cannot move. Your body has become the binding. Stone beneath your feet cools, hardening around you. The ritual ground seals itself, the fractures knitting not with flexibility but with permanence. The last echoes of thunder fade into silence so complete it feels reverent.

Druin approaches slowly, fear warring with awe in his eyes. He stops several paces away. He cannot come closer. The air around you hums with restrained force, invisible but absolute. Even standing near you feels like pressing against the edge of a storm that refuses to break. "What have you done?" he whispers. You try to answer. No sound comes. Not because your voice is gone—but because speech would require movement, and movement would fracture the containment. You understand this instinctively now. Your body is no longer yours to command freely. It is a structure. A seal. A cage.

Druin understands without words. His shoulders sag, grief and reverence intertwining until they are indistinguishable. He kneels—not to worship, but to acknowledge what has been sacrificed. "They will remember you," he says hoarsely. "They will warn their children." You watch him leave, his figure growing smaller against the newly calm sky.

You watch generations pass. Time behaves strangely around you. Days blur into
seasons. Seasons into years. Your awareness does not drift or dull, but it changes
scale. You feel the land the way you once
felt your own breath—subtle shifts in pressure, distant tremors of unrest, the slow,
patient growth of forests where devastation once reigned.

People come. At first, they come in
fear—approaching cautiously, leaving offerings at the edge of the ritual ground,
whispering prayers they do not expect answered. Later, they come in awe, telling
stories of the one who bound the storm
and became its prison. They build stones
around you. Not walls. Markers. They
leave space, understanding instinctively
that containment requires distance. The
site becomes a place of warning rather
than blessing. Children are brought here to
learn not courage, but consequence. "This
is where control ends," elders say. "This is
where power stays put."

Kings come, eventually. They do not
approach closely. They study you from

afar, measuring what it would mean to rule a land that no longer fears divine storms—but remembers what happens when mortals try to own them. Some kings govern more carefully after seeing you. Others harden, convinced they can avoid your fate by never reaching too far.

The storm inside you never sleeps. It presses constantly, testing, measuring, seeking release that will never be granted. You feel its movements as tension rather than pain now, an endless coiled force held in perfect balance. You learn how to absorb its surges, how to distribute strain through your immobile form so the land does not feel it. You are no longer a person. You are infrastructure. Memory fades differently than you feared. Not erased—but compressed, distilled into meaning rather than detail. Faces blur. Names dissolve. But purpose remains sharp as ever. Hold. Contain. Endure.

Centuries pass. The world changes around you. Borders shift. Languages evolve. Gods fade into story, then into metaphor. The storm remains locked behind your will, unable to devour memory, unable to reclaim dominion. You become myth while still existing. Travelers stand at a distance and swear they feel watched—not by you, but by the storm you keep from them. Some claim they hear thunder deep beneath the ground on quiet nights, as if the sky itself remembers what you are holding. You do not answer. You do not forgive. You simply remain. In time, even Druin becomes legend. Only the stones remember his name.

One day—long after anyone expects it—the storm presses harder than it ever has. Not in rebellion. In exhaustion. You understand then what eternity truly costs. The storm will never escape. But neither will you. The land has stabilized, yes—but at the price of a single, unyielding point where change is forbidden. You are a warning etched into the world: proof that absolute control is possible, and that it demands an absolute sacrifice.

The sky above you remains calm. Too calm. Perfectly obedient. And in that obedience, something fragile is lost forever.

You stand immobile beneath a sky that will never challenge itself again. A living seal. A silent cage. A cataclysm denied expression by your endless restraint. This is the ending you chose. Not release. Not renewal. Containment without end. And Ériu endures—safe, scarred, and forever shaped by the figure who became the storm's prison so the world would never have to.

# Chapter 35
# Dominion of Fractured Skies

YOU DO NOT TURN away. You step forward into the pressure left behind by the storm's fracture and claim it as unfinished work. The air shivers when you move, as if the land itself recognizes the decision before you speak it aloud. The storm-shards are no longer a distant problem; they are vectors—forces seeking shape. You give them one. Not freedom. Not release. Structure. You begin where the fracture is loudest.

On the northern forest's edge, lightning still crawls through bark and root, the sky sagging with static. You raise your hands—not in communion, not in surrender—and the fragments respond. They recognize the authority that shaped their division. Pressure bends toward you. Wind straightens. The storm's erratic pulses tighten into rhythm. You do not absorb the shards. You arrange them.

With sigils drawn into earth and air alike, you anchor the first fragment into a lattice of containment—pillars of pressure mapped across the canopy, channels that redirect force downward and outward, never allowing it to pool or surge. Thunder quiets to a controlled cadence. Rain falls when needed. The forest still crackles with energy, but it no longer lashes indiscriminately. The land steadies.

You repeat the work along the western coast. Where the sea once surged unpredictably, you set storm-anchors beneath the waves, binding wind to tide, lightning to depth. Harbors reform. Routes stabilize. Sailors learn the rules quickly: follow the markers, obey the signals, do not test the margins. The storms obey.

In the mountains, the work is hardest. Clouds cling stubbornly to stone, thunder echoing endlessly through passes carved by ages of pressure. You climb anyway, carving law into cliff-face and sky, shaping conduits that bleed excess force into the rock itself. Peaks glow faintly at night, etched with a geometry no one fully understands. When the last anchor locks into place, the sky exhales. Ériu becomes quiet. Not empty. Not peaceful. Regulated.

Druin finds you weeks later, standing beneath a sky that no longer surprises itself. He studies the horizon, where clouds gather into clean, predictable layers, where thunder waits politely for permission. "You have done it," he says. There is no admiration in his voice. No accusation either. Only certainty. "The storms answer to pattern now." "They answer to law," you reply. He nods slowly. "And law answers to you." You do not deny it.

The land stabilizes swiftly. Crops thrive in regions once battered by erratic weather. Roads reopen. Trade resumes with confidence rather than hope. Floods recede into managed channels. Droughts are countered by controlled release from cloud and wind. Kings rejoice. Councils praise. Shrines rise—not to gods, but to systems. Stone circles etched with storm-geometry stand at crossroads and coastlines alike, tended by wardens trained to read pressure and signal shifts long before danger arrives. The old fear returns, transformed. Not fear of divine whim—but fear of deviation.

Rules emerge quickly. Storm-zones are mapped. Travel permits required. Construction codes enforced. Regions that once adapted organically to their skies now adapt to standards handed down from central authority. Disobedience is not punished by lightning—but by denial of protection. Those who live outside the lattice feel it most. Storms still gather beyond the anchors, wild and restless, slamming against invisible boundaries. Communities at the edges suffer harder impacts, their skies compressed into narrower margins. Complaints rise. Petitions follow. You answer some. You ignore others.

You tell yourself this is necessary. A system must have edges to function. You establish the Conclave of Skyward Law—a body tasked with maintaining the anchors, enforcing compliance, adjudicating disputes over storm-access and weather rights. They consult you often at first. Less so as procedures harden into doctrine.

Your presence becomes ceremonial. Necessary. Untouchable.

Children grow up learning the rules before the stories. They memorize the patterns of allowed storms, the signs that indicate lawful rain or sanctioned thunder. They are taught that unpredictability is dangerous, that the old world nearly broke beneath it. They are not taught that it also grew.

As years pass, the anchors become sacred—not because they are divine, but because they are indispensable. No one remembers how to live without them. No one wants to. Those who challenge the system are not struck down. They are cut off. Denied access to regulated skies, forced to live beneath the pressure at the margins. Some adapt. Many leave. A few resist openly—and are made examples of, their regions brought forcefully back into compliance as storms are redirected away from their lands.

The sky remains calm. Too calm. You feel it in your bones—the tension of power held in check, stretched thin across an entire country. The storm-shards strain constantly against their containment, not to escape, but to move. Motion is their nature. You have turned it into obedience.

At Tara, the stones remain cracked but silent. The Lia Fáil does not glow. It does not cry out. It has been rendered obsolete by a more efficient truth. You return there once, standing beneath a sky that looks painted rather than lived-in. Druin joins you, older now, his eyes sharper for what has been lost. "The land endures," he says. "But it no longer remembers how to argue with itself." You look out across Ériu—stable, prosperous, quiet. "Argument is costly," you answer. "So is silence," he replies. He leaves shortly after. Some say he walks beyond the anchors, into the unregulated skies, seeking what remains of the old storms. Others say he simply fades, unable to reconcile himself to a world that no longer needs dissent to survive. You remain.

You do not age the way others do anymore. The lattice ties you to the system, feeds you longevity in exchange for vigilance. You become less a ruler than a cornerstone—necessary, immovable, unquestioned. Generations pass. No god challenges your dominion. The storm does not rebel. The prophecy remains shattered, irrelevant, its fragments locked into function rather than meaning.

Ériu becomes efficient. Predictable. Enduring. And brittle. On rare nights, when the anchors hum louder than usual, you sense the storm-shards pressing—not to escape, but to change. You tighten the system, adjust parameters, reinforce containment. You tell yourself that flexibility can be engineered later. That mercy can be added. That dissent can be managed. The sky above remains obedient. The land below bends. This is the ending you chose. Not freedom. Not devastation. Stability imposed by will and maintained through unyielding law. Ériu endures—orderly, controlled, and shaped forever by the hand that refused to let the sky decide for itself.

# Chapter 36
## The Iron Crown

THE SKY DOES NOT fall silent all at once. At first, it merely stops answering. Storms still come, but they arrive without warning and depart without meaning—no crow circles before the flood. No dream stirs ahead of fire. The old signs fade into superstition, then into mockery. What once guided becomes something to be conquered—or ignored. And into that quiet, human voices rush.

The first rulers of this age are cautious. They speak of reason and reform, of replacing prophecy with law. They promise stability where gods once meddled, clarity where omens once confused. Their laws are careful at first, shaped by consensus and necessity. People welcome them. After all, the storms no longer choose favorites. Someone must. But power, once unobserved by sky or stone, learns quickly.

Without prophecy, legitimacy must be manufactured. Without divine witness, authority must be displayed. Crowns grow heavier, forged not of gold but of iron—practical, unadorned, unmistakable. Symbols change. Banners replace blessings. Oaths are sworn not to land or god, but to the ruler who commands the most force to enforce them. The old shrines are repurposed. Some become armories. Others become treasuries. A few become stages where rulers speak of destiny with a practiced irony, borrowing the language of the gods they no longer fear. "Fate," they say, smiling thinly, "is what we make it."

Technology advances quickly here, too—but not evenly. Knowledge is hoarded rather than shared. Medicine is developed first for soldiers. Engineering is applied to fortifications before homes. Where the Age of Hands and Minds built networks of care, this age builds chains of command. Efficiency becomes virtue. Mercy becomes weakness. War returns—not as ritual, not as defense against divine wrath, but as policy.

The first great conflict of the Iron Crown is brief and decisive. A neighboring region resists annexation. Their leaders appeal to old customs, to shared history, to the memory of balance between land and people. The response is swift. Weapons break walls that once would have stood against any storm. The victory is celebrated as proof that gods were never necessary. The land remembers nothing. That, too, becomes proof.

More rulers follow. Some are brilliant. Some are cruel. Most are both. Each claims to bring order where chaos once ruled. Each leaves behind scars that no prophecy rises to condemn. Without a higher law to contradict them, every decision becomes defensible if it succeeds. And when it fails, there is no one left to blame but enemies.

Storms worsen. Not because they are angry, but because the world is changing in ways no one pauses to understand. Forests are cleared for expansion. Rivers are forced into channels too narrow to hold them. Mountains are cut open for what lies beneath. When floods come, rulers call them unfortunate accidents. When droughts arrive, they are blamed on rival states. The sky does not intervene. People begin to miss the gods—not because the gods were kind, but because they were limits. Once, there had been lines rulers could not cross without fear of consequence. Once, there had been forces that reminded even kings they were small.

Now there is only escalation. Weapons grow louder. Borders harden. Alliances shift and fracture, bound not by shared survival but by temporary advantage. One tyrant falls to rebellion, replaced by another who promises restraint and delivers retribution. History accelerates, each decade more violent than the last.

Scholars attempt warnings. They write of imbalance, of consequences deferred too long. They speak of storms no longer guided, of land stripped beyond recovery. Some are listened to. Most are ignored. Their work is shelved, censored, or weaponized—turned into strategies rather than cautions. A new doctrine takes hold: Control is peace. If the land rebels, control it. If people dissent, control them. If the future threatens uncertainty, control the narrative. Iron replaces ritual.

The greatest empire of this age builds a capital where Tara once stood sacred. The standing stones are dismantled, their fragments used to pave ceremonial roads. The Lia Fáil is broken apart and displayed as an artifact—proof that the old world has been conquered. Tour guides recite sanitized myths to visitors who laugh politely and move on. Above the capital, storms gather more frequently now. Not as an omen. As pressure.

Lightning strikes towers and is redirected by metal spines thrust proudly skyward. Floods breach walls built too close to rivers. Fires spread faster than response systems can manage. Each disaster is answered with greater force, greater extraction, greater insistence that control will eventually overcome consequence. It never does.

There comes a war that historians later call Inevitable—because no one can agree when it truly began. It consumes multiple regions, fueled by grievances layered too thick to unravel. Cities burn. Supply lines collapse. Refugees flood borders that close in their faces. The Iron Crown changes hands twice during the conflict, each successor more ruthless than the last. And still, the sky does nothing. Some whisper that this is the gods' revenge. Others insist it proves the gods never existed at all. Neither explanation helps. The world is now governed by momentum alone.

Near the end, a child stands on a hill where the stones once spoke. The child watches a distant storm roll across the horizon—vast, indifferent, unclaimed. It does not listen. It does not wait. It simply passes, leaving ruin where it must and calm where it may. The child asks an elder why the storms never warn anyone anymore. The elder, weary and scarred, answers honestly. "Because no one taught them how."

The story ends without judgment from the sky. There is no god to devour the world. No prophecy to fulfill or avert. No seer to interpret the signs. There is only humanity—armed, ambitious, and unchecked—ruling beneath a silent heaven.

The Iron Crown endures, reforged again and again, each ruler convinced they will be the last necessary tyrant. The land bears the weight until it cannot bear it any longer. When collapse finally comes, it will not arrive as myth. It will arrive as consequence. Until that time arrives, the sky watches no longer, and the crown remains.

# Chapter 37
## The Shattered Prophesy

THE STONE GOES QUIET beneath your hand. Not sleeping and not waiting. Finished. When you lift your palm from the fractured runes, the last echo of the old law fades like breath against cold glass. The chamber beneath the hall feels smaller, as though the stone itself has drawn inward, relieved to be spared further remembrance. The hum that once pressed against your bones is gone. In its place is a neat, obedient stillness—the kind that follows a door being closed and barred.

Druin exhales slowly. Relief crosses his face first. Then dread, as if he has realized relief is only another word for postponement. "It's done," he says. You nod. You do not look back at the broken standing stone. You know better now than to linger over what has been buried.

Above, the hall stands. Maelchon's reign continues. The torches still burn. The benches still hold. The crown remains slightly askew—but it stays on his head, and that is enough. Whatever sickness lies beneath the rule of kings, it will not be cured tonight. Order holds. The world does not fracture. And somewhere far above stone and soil, the storm listens.

At first, nothing seems to change. Messengers ride. Laws are spoken. Oaths are sworn and enforced with familiar rituals. Druids return to their places beside thrones, advising where they can, silent where they must. The Lia Fáil remains cracked, its hum reduced to a memory felt only by those who once stood too close to its truth.

The prophecy—what remains of it—no longer pulls at you. Its fragments drift apart, no longer aligning into warning or promise. You realize, slowly, with a cold clarity that settles in your chest, that the prophecy has not been delayed. It has been broken.

Without the old law restored and without the land's voice fully awakened, the storm has no path to negotiation. No doorway shaped by truth. No boundary that says this far and no further. It gathers anyway. Storms always do.

The first signs come as absence. Divine silence spreads across Ériu like an unspoken decree. Oracles dream nothing. Sacred wells lose their edge. Offerings rot where once they burned clean. When people pray, they hear only their own voices echo back. Some rejoice. "No gods to judge us," Maelchon declares in open council. "No ancient whims to bind our hands. We will govern ourselves." And for a time, it works.

Man-made law blossoms where divine guidance once loomed. Councils refine codes—kings issue decrees. Systems of justice are argued, rewritten, improved. In some regions, fairness grows stronger without the fear of divine reprisal. People learn, slowly, painfully, how to weigh mercy against order without looking to the sky for permission.

In other places, cruelty finds new shelter. Without sacred limits, punishment hardens. Power consolidates. Kings decide they answer only to precedent and steel. The land does not object. It no longer knows how.

You watch all of this from the margins, no longer called seer with the same reverence. Without prophecy, your sight dims—not vanishing, but narrowing to the scale of human consequence. You are no longer a hinge upon which gods might turn. You are simply someone who remembers what was almost said.

Druin visits you once, years later, his hair gone gray, his shoulders bent beneath responsibility he never wanted. "We are alone now," he tells you. "Do you know that?" You do.

The storm comes without warning, not as a single cataclysm, but as a devouring season. Storms rise where they never rose before. Winds scour coastlines into bone. Rain falls too hard or not at all. Lightning strikes sacred places first—as if drawn to the last faint residues of divine presence—and shatters them into silence. People look to kings. Kings look to laws. Laws hold—for a while. But the storm is no god. It does not bargain. It does not accept sacrifice. It does not listen. It consumes.

The first god it devours is memory. Old myths stop being told accurately. Names blur. Stories lose their endings. Children grow up hearing fragments of legends that no longer resolve into meaning. Even the Ancestral Chorus fades—not silenced by force, but starved of remembrance.

Then the land itself begins to change. Forests die where they once endured storms. Rivers alter course with no regard for boundary stones. Crops fail unpredictably. The soil does not curse anyone—it simply does not care. You realize, too late, that by sealing the old law, you did not preserve balance. You removed the last language the land had to speak back to catastrophe.

When the storm finally reveals its full shape, it is not crowned. It does not wear the masks of gods or kings. It is vast, formless, indifferent—a pressure system without intent, a force that has devoured divinity and found no resistance worth acknowledging. It does not kneel. It does not rage theatrically. It simply moves.

Cities are abandoned not because they fall, but because survival migrates. Borders lose meaning. Kings still rule, issuing edicts to fewer and fewer subjects, their authority shrinking to the walls they can defend. Some rulers adapt, governing wisely within human limits. Others cling to titles that echo in empty halls.

The prophecy does not return. There is no final choice. No destined confrontation. No godborn reckoning shaped by mortal will. The prophecy died the moment you buried the law that could have carried it. You understand now what a prophecy truly is—not a promise of salvation, but a conversation—a warning spoken across generations, requiring both sides to listen. You ended the conversation. In the end, Ériu becomes a land governed entirely by people.

Some communities thrive through cooperation and memory. Others collapse into cycles of exploitation and retreat. There is no single ending written across the island—only many small stories, some hopeful, some brutal, all disconnected from the sky.

You grow old. Not slowly. Not anchored by divine consequence. Just old. On your final journey to Tara, the hill feels like any other rise of land. The standing stones remain, weathered and inert, their cracks filled with moss rather than light. Ravens still perch there, but they are only birds now. You kneel beside the Lia Fáil and place your hand on cold stone. It does not answer.

In that silence, you finally understand the cost of what you chose to preserve: A world free of divine tyranny. A world free of divine guidance. A world where every law is made by human hands—and must bear the full weight of human failure.

The storm rolls overhead, distant and uncaring. Not a god. Not a judge. Just weather. The prophecy is gone and not fulfilled. Not averted. Shattered. And Ériu endures—not because it was chosen, but because it learned, alone, how to survive what was never meant to listen. This is the end you have made. A world without destiny. A world with only consequences.

# Chapter 38
# The Veiled Law

YOU DO NOT RISE from the broken stone quickly. The Law Chamber is quiet now—too quiet, as though the air itself has learned restraint. Where moments ago the fractured runes hummed with the pressure of choice, they now lie still beneath your palm, their lines altered in ways no eye but yours could fully trace. You did not restore what was lost. You did not finish the erasure begun generations ago. You did something far more dangerous. You taught the law how to hide.

The land's authority breathes again, but it does so behind a veil—its voice muffled, its judgments indirect. Power will no longer answer cleanly to crown or oath. It will seep instead, withdrawing from those who strain it too far, unraveling certainty without ever naming the reason. Kings will fall without knowing why. Rulers will hesitate, sensing weakness where none can be proven. The law will no longer accuse. It will withhold.

You lift your hand. The stone does not cry out. It does not answer. And yet, deep beneath Tara, something settles—patient, alert, and waiting. You turn from the chamber as footsteps echo softly on the stairs. Druin descends alone this time. His face is pale in the torchlight, eyes narrowed not in fear, but in calculation. He kneels beside the stone without touching it, studying the runes with the care of one who knows better than to assume silence means absence. "You didn't restore it," he says at last. "No," you reply. After a pause, he says, "You didn't destroy it either." Again, you reply, "No."

Druin exhales slowly, as though setting something heavy down inside himself. "You've bound it to consequence without confession," he murmurs. "Kings will feel it—but never see it." You respond, "That was the intent."

He looks up at you then, searching your face for something—certainty, perhaps, or doubt. He finds neither. "They'll call it chance," he says. "Or fate. Or bad seasons. They'll invent reasons to avoid naming what they can't control." You agree. "And when the wrong king falls?" he asks quietly. "When a careful one is undone alongside the cruel?" You meet his gaze without flinching. "The land has always been indifferent to fairness. Only to balance." Druin nods once. He does not argue. That, more than anything, tells you he understands the cost of what you've done.

You ascend the stairs together. The stone door grinds open above, releasing the scent of smoke and timber and human breath. Maelchon waits near the threshold, his posture easy, his expression unreadable. He studies your faces closely, as if expecting to see some mark of upheaval. "Well?" he asks. "Did you find what you were looking for?" You incline your head—not in submission, not in challenge, but in acknowledgment. "The chamber remains sealed." Relief flickers across his face before he can suppress it. "Good," he says. "Then we are done here." Perhaps. For now.

The hall above resumes its uneasy rhythm. Cups are refilled. Laughter rises—brittle, persistent, forced into shape by habit rather than ease. Life continues here, unaware of how subtly it has been altered. You stand among them like a stone set beneath the floorboards—unseen, bearing weight, supporting a structure that will never acknowledge what holds it upright.

You leave the hall before dawn. Not in secrecy. Not in exile. Simply, without ceremony. The guards do not stop you. The doors open as they always have. Outside, the night air is cool and unremarkable, carrying no omen, no warning. Only when the hill rises beneath your feet, and Tara's stones come into view, does the land seem to register your passing. They remain cracked but quiet, their light dimmed to memory. No prophecy stirs. No storm answers your departure. The world has accepted your choice—and folded it inward.

Years pass. At first, the changes are imperceptible. A king grows ill without cause. A favored heir falters where no weakness was known. A harsh decree fails to take root, ignored by land and people alike. Scholars argue. Priests mutter. Advisors whisper of omens no one can agree upon.

Maelchon rules carefully. He has learned restraint, sensing the limits closing around him even if he cannot name them. His successors are less fortunate. Some fall swiftly. Others endure only by tempering their ambition, discovering—without ever being told—that power no longer answers as it once did. The land does not rebel. It does not rise. It corrects. Communities adapt. Leadership becomes provisional, fragile, contingent. Those who rule learn to listen—not to gods, not to prophecy, but to the subtle resistance of soil and season. There are no great revolutions. No clean reckoning. Only adjustment, followed by survival.

You walk Ériu's length and breadth, watching the effects ripple outward. You do not intervene. You do not explain. To do so would be to unmask the law—and once seen, it could be named, resisted, broken again. Some nights, you dream of the chamber beneath Tara. Of runes shifting quietly when no one is looking. Of a law that remembers your hand and waits for it to return.

Druin visits you once, many years later. He is older now, his hair silvered, his movements slower. He brings no accusation. "They're calling it the Quiet Failing," he tells you over a low fire. "Power that simply... slips. No curse. No sign. Just absence." You nod. "Names help people endure uncertainty." Druin states, "They want to know if it can be fixed." You stare into the flames. "It was never meant to be fixed."

Druin studies you for a long moment. "And you?" he asks. "Do you regret it?" You consider the question carefully. You think of the chaos you prevented. The tyranny you forestalled. The truths you buried so deeply that they may never surface again. "No," you say at last. "But I won't pretend it was clean." He accepts that. He always has.

When he leaves, you are alone again—one witness among many who will never know what you carry. You have not saved Ériu. You have not redeemed it. You have not ruled it. You have tilted it.

The future will belong to those who learn to live within limits they cannot see. There will be injustice. There will be suffering. But there will also be endurance—slow, stubborn, and unremarkable. The land no longer cries out for kings. And no one will ever quite understand why. This is the price of compromise.

# Chapter 39
## The Age of Many Skies

YOU TURN AWAY. NOT in exhaustion. Not in fear. But in refusal. The storm-fragments churn across Ériu's horizons—three, four, sometimes more skies moving with different tempers and hungers. You feel them still, faintly, like pressure changes before weather breaks. They wait for you to impose meaning, to draw lines, to finish what you began. You do not. You let your hands fall to your sides. You step back from the place where authority would take root and choose absence over dominion. The rite's residue fades around you, leaving scorched stone and cooling air. The storm does not protest. It simply continues.

Druin watches you in silence. He has seen you bind. He has seen you unbind. This, he understands, is something else entirely. "You are leaving it unfinished," he says at last. "No," you answer. "I am leaving it alive."

The storm-fragments remain unmoored. Not united. Not destroyed. Not governed. They settle where momentum and chance carry them, becoming local truths rather than a single destiny. Ériu does not fracture cleanly—it diversifies, the land answering each fragment differently, unevenly, without consensus.

In the eastern plains, storms come suddenly and pass just as fast. Rain lashes hard, then vanishes, leaving fields richer but harder to predict. Farmers adapt or fail depending on how quickly they learn the new rhythms. Old calendars lose relevance. New signs are watched—cloud tilt, wind taste, the way birds lift from grass before thunder arrives.

Along the northern forests, lightning becomes a season rather than an event. Trees grow thick bark and twisted crowns. Fires spark often but burn fast, clearing undergrowth and making space for stubborn green life. People there become watchers of the sky, neither worshipping nor fearing it, but reading it the way one reads a dangerous neighbor's moods.

The western coasts grow wild. Storm-surges reshape shorelines year by year, opening coves and swallowing others. Fishing villages relocate often, rebuilding lightly, learning not to cling too hard to one place. Sailors speak of waters that remember storms long after clouds have passed, currents that turn without warning.

In the high mountains, thunder never truly leaves. Clouds cling low, sound echoing endlessly through stone corridors. Those who live there become quiet folk, careful with words and gestures, believing sound itself draws attention. They build inward, deep into rock, and say the sky listens even when it does not strike.

Ériu becomes a land of many skies. There is no single pattern to master. No authority to petition. No prophecy to complete. The old idea of balance—one storm, one rule, one ending—dies quietly, not in failure but in irrelevance.

Kings struggle first. Without divine signs or unified weather to legitimize rule, authority becomes regional and fragile. Some kings fall quickly, unable to govern lands that behave differently from valley to valley. Others adapt, ceding power, forming councils, negotiating with communities shaped by storms that refuse uniformity. A few try force. They do not last. Armies cannot march through weather that shifts by the mile. Supply lines fail. Sieges dissolve when storms isolate cities unpredictably. Control becomes local, conditional, temporary.

Law changes too. Instead of a single code, traditions multiply. What is forbidden under one sky is tolerated under another. Justice becomes contextual, argued rather than enforced by precedent. This breeds conflict—but also resilience. People learn to negotiate difference rather than erase it.

Stories change. Bards stop singing of the Seer who saved or doomed the world. Instead, they tell smaller tales: of villages lost and rebuilt, of storms survived by chance and skill, of generations who learned the signs their grandparents ignored. Your name survives in fragments. Some remember you as the one who refused to finish the storm. Others call you coward, visionary, fool. Children hear half-true stories of a figure who could have ruled the sky and chose not to. You do not correct them.

You walk. You travel Ériu for years, seeing what your choice has made possible—and what it has broken. You help where you can, not as authority but as witness. You warn some villages when storms gather. You leave others to learn the hard way. You age. The faint ache of storm-pressure never fully leaves your bones, but it no longer pulls at you with purpose. You are not a conduit. Not a cage. Not a crown. Just a person who stepped aside.

Druin records what he can, though his writings grow increasingly contradictory. One region thrives under wild skies. Another collapses beneath the same forces. He stops trying to reconcile the accounts. "There is no single truth anymore," he says one evening as you watch clouds move in opposite directions overhead. "That is the truth," you reply. Eventually, even Druin settles, choosing a place where storms pass often but not violently. He dies old, content, surrounded by people who remember him not as a druid of authority, but as one who listened.

Years later, you return to Tara. The hill is quiet. The standing stones remain cracked, their glow long gone. Moss fills the fissures. Grass grows thick around their bases. Ravens still come, but they do not linger. The Lia Fáil is just a stone now—weathered, silent, irrelevant. You stand at the center of the ring and feel... nothing answer. No chorus. No pressure. No expectation. The land does not hold its breath.

Storms move on distant horizons—three directions at once tonight—but none gather here. Tara is no longer a center. It is a memory. You kneel, resting your hand against cool stone. For the first time since the prophecy shattered, you understand that the world does not require an ending to continue. It only requires people willing to live without one. You leave Tara at dawn.

Behind you, the hill remains—no longer a throne, no longer a warning. Ahead, roads diverge endlessly beneath shifting skies. The Age of Many Skies has begun. There will be suffering. There will be beauty. There will be no single voice claiming to know which is which. And Ériu endures—not because it was saved, not because it was controlled, but because it was allowed to change unevenly, stubbornly, and honestly. This is the ending you chose. Not dominion. Not collapse. A world that must learn itself again and again—beneath many heavens. The storm moves on. So do you.

# Chapter 40
# The Controlled Ending Path

YOU FINISH THE ERASURE with steady hands. The last line of rune-light fades beneath your palm, swallowed by stone as if it has been hungry for silence. The Law Chamber exhales—not with relief, but with restraint. The hum that once rose through bedrock and bone recedes until the air feels smaller, contained, obedient. Your torch burns more cleanly now, its flame no longer tugged sideways by unseen pressure.

The land has not forgiven what you have done. It has simply stopped pressing. You stand and listen. There is no answer. Not from the old law. Not from the stones. Not from the ancestral chorus that once thinned the air with murmurs. Only the quiet of a room designed to be forgotten, and the faint drip of water that has been falling here since before Maelchon ever wore a crown. In your pouch, the Oath-Stone Fragment—once warm, once eager—cools to dull weight. It feels like a tooth pulled clean from the jaw of the world. Not gone, but removed from its true place.

Above, footsteps echo. The sound travels down the stairs like a slow verdict, though no verdict has been spoken. You extinguish one torch and take the other, leaving the chamber in darkness. The darkness does not resist. It welcomes itself.

When you climb the hidden stairs back toward the king's hall, each step feels easier than it should. The stone no longer seems to watch you. The air no longer bears the subtle charge of judgment. You realize with a small, sharp chill that this is what Maelchon wanted most—not your loyalty, not your skill, not even your silence. He wanted the land to stop listening.

The stairs open behind a hanging tapestry. You slip through it like a thought that must not be spoken aloud. The hall's hearths burn low, and most of the warriors sleep in uneasy heaps of wool and bone-tired limbs. A few remain awake, drinking quietly, eyes flicking toward you and away again. In their gaze is something new: not reverence, not suspicion, but a kind of instinctive caution, like livestock sensing a gate has been shut.

Maelchon is waiting. Not at the high seat. Not in grandeur. He stands near the far end of the hall where shadows gather between pillars, his cloak loose, his crown absent. Without it, he looks almost ordinary—except for his eyes, which hold the steady confidence of a man who believes the world has agreed to his terms. "You found what you sought," he says softly. You do not answer with words. Words would imply an exchange. This was never an exchange. It was a surrender dressed in necessity.

Maelchon's gaze drifts over your hands, lingering where your palm bears faint traces of stone-dust. "And you understood," he continues, "why some things must remain... beneath." You meet his eyes. In that moment, you consider saying the truth—that you did not understand so much as you chose, and that every choice has a taste, and this one tastes of iron and sealed doors. But you have already given him silence once. It would be foolish to pretend you are not capable of giving it again. "I understood the cost," you say at last.

A smile flickers at the corner of his mouth, small as a knife-tip. "Good." He does not threaten you. He does not need to. Threats are for those who still believe they have to persuade the world into obedience. Maelchon believes obedience is the natural state of things if one only removes the sources of interruption. He steps closer. "You will remain here," he says, not as a command but as an assumption. "You have seen what lies beneath my hall. You will not wander into another lord's court with that knowledge on your tongue."

You could refuse. You could leave this hall, slip into the night, and run before his reach tightens around you. But you feel the land tonight—how quiet it has become, how neatly it has folded itself. The old path of resistance is not gone, but it is dulled. The world will no longer rise to meet a challenge. It will not instinctively tilt toward justice. If you leave, you will be one lone seer on lonely roads, carrying truth that no longer has a living root. You nod once. Maelchon's relief is so slight it is almost invisible. He turns away, and the matter is settled.

In the days that follow, the hall brightens, not with joy, but with confidence. Warriors laugh more easily. Courtiers speak louder. Messengers arrive with reports from across Ériu, and none of them carry the strange, tremor-laced language of land-rebukes or omen-signs. The storms behave. The stones remain inert. The Lia Fáil does not cry, does not crack further, does not punish. The people feel it and misname it. They call it peace. They call it prosperity. They call Maelchon's rule strong, blessed, inevitable.

Maelchon begins issuing new laws—clear, practical, human-made. Some are sensible. He strengthens roads. He standardizes measures. He curbs a few feuds by enforcing consistent penalties rather than letting rival clans spill blood for generations. Trade improves. Markets grow. There is a tangible relief in the countryside, the kind that comes when people believe the ground beneath them will not suddenly open its mouth. But the relief has an edge.

The old rituals diminish. Druids are welcomed less for wisdom and more for ceremony. Oaths are spoken quickly, without the old trembling caution, because the land does not weigh them anymore. Promises become language rather than binding. It is easier to lie when the world has stopped flinching at dishonesty.

And while Maelchon's laws begin to spread, so do other laws—made by other hands, in other halls, without sacred measure to restrain ambition. In some regions, lords copy Maelchon's steadier decrees and govern fairly. In others, they sharpen their codes into weapons and call it order. Ériu becomes governed not by omens, not by land-judgment, but by human appetite—sometimes generous, often hungry. You feel the shift as a change in the air, subtle as the difference between fresh water and salted. The world has begun to speak in a new tongue. The old tongue is not dead. It is simply unused, like a blade buried under a hearthstone.

Druin does not stay. He remains long enough to watch Maelchon's confidence harden into habit. He sees how the court leans into comfort, how truth becomes an inconvenience rather than a compass. He speaks to you once, in the early dawn, when the hall still sleeps, and the hearths are only embers. "You've bought time," he says quietly. His eyes are tired. "That's all. Time is not absolution." "What would you have done?" you ask.

Druin looks toward the hall's pillars, as if he can see through them into the buried chamber below. "I would have let the land speak," he says. "Even if it screamed." "And if the scream broke Ériu?" You ask. "Then at least it would be Ériu breaking honestly," he replies.

He leaves before midday, taking no escort, carrying only his staff and whatever grief he refuses to name. Later, someone says they saw him at the edge of a bog, speaking to reeds like they could answer. Someone else swears he walked north into storm country and never returned. His absence becomes a rumor, then a caution, then a footnote.

You remain. Not because you believe in Maelchon. Not because you have surrendered to him. But because you understand the shape of what you have become: a keeper of a buried truth, a witness who cannot easily become a herald. Maelchon uses you without openly using you. When disputes arise that smell faintly of omen or ancestral claim, he consults you privately, extracting only what is useful. He never asks for prophecy. He asks for advantage. And you answer—sometimes with clarity, sometimes with careful vagueness—constantly aware that each word you release might tighten the knot you have tied around Ériu's throat.

Years pass. The hall grows grander. The kingdom grows tidier. Taxes become reliable. Armies march efficiently. Maelchon is praised as a ruler who brought stability after an age of cracks and storms. Yet beneath the tidy surface, you notice what begins to wither. Small dissent. Local traditions. The wildness of communities shaping themselves without approval.

People grow cautious—not because the gods demand it, but because law demands it, and law is now only as merciful as those who enforce it. Some villages thrive under fair codes. Others suffocate under rigid ones. There is no sacred counterweight. No land-voice to reject corruption. No stone that cries out beneath a liar's foot.

One winter, you travel beyond Tara's reach—quietly, with Maelchon's permission couched in a dozen polite constraints—and you see the truth in the countryside. On the surface: order. Crops stored. Roads maintained. Watchmen posted. Underneath: fear of punishment that is not always just. A resignation that feels like surrender. A tiredness not of bodies, but of spirits.

A farmer speaks to you in whispers while snow falls softly around the thatch-roofed huts. "It's quieter," they say. "That's what folk wanted. Quiet." "And do you have it?" you ask. They look toward the dark line of forest where the wind moves through branches. "Mostly," they admit. "But sometimes I miss the old feeling—that the land cared enough to notice us."

You return to Tara at spring's edge, climbing the hill alone at dawn. The standing stones are mist-wet, their fissures mossed over. The Lia Fáil stands unchanged—cracked but inert, as if it has accepted its own silencing. You place your hand against it—cold stone. No hum. No chorus. A raven watches from a distant stone, head tilted as if listening for something that does not come.

For a long moment, you stand there and feel the truth settle into you like a second spine: You did not end the storm. You did not heal the land. You merely removed the land's ability to answer. The prophecy does not return. It does not complete itself. It does not fulfill or fail in any glorious fashion. It simply fades, its shards dulled by disuse, its warning lost in the machinery of human governance. And perhaps that is the most unsettling ending of all. No apocalypse. No triumph. Just continuation.

Maelchon rules. Then another rules. Then another. Laws improve in some places, rot in others. Ériu endures through human effort and human cruelty, through decisions that are no longer weighed by anything beyond mortal consequence. The debt you buried remains buried for now. But you know how stone behaves. You know how pressure collects. You know how silence is never empty—only waiting.

You leave Tara at dawn, walking down the hill as mist curls around your ankles like fingers that almost remember how to hold you. Behind you, the stones stand mute. Ahead, Ériu turns beneath a sky that no longer offers judgment—only weather, only time, only the long, slow return of consequences. This is the ending you chose—a world held together by restraint. A truth buried deep enough to last. A stability purchased with silence— and paid for, steadily, in the years to come.

# Chapter 41
## The Unseen Age

YOU DO NOT BARGAIN with your blood. You do not plead with it, coax it, ask it to become gentle. You take hold of the Ancestral Thread the way one takes hold of a thorn that has been left too long beneath the skin—knowing it will hurt, knowing it must come out, knowing the wound will be worse if you pretend it is not there.

The storm gathers above you in slow spirals, patient as stone. Lightning sketches pale, deliberate arcs within the cloud-body, as if the sky is writing in a language only your marrow can read. The Ancestral Chorus swells, their voices braided into lament and exultation, singing names that taste like iron and hearth-smoke and old grief. They expect you to ascend. They expect you to become the axis. Instead, you turn inward, not toward power, but toward the principle beneath it.

The Ancestral Thread is not a cord you can cut with a blade. It is not a knot you can untie with clever hands. It is a law written into flesh—an inheritance older than kings, older than the stones of Tara, older than the first human who looked at lightning and called it divine.

You find it by listening to your own pulse. It hums beneath your skin, bright and terrible, a vibration that matches the storm's pressure exactly. You follow the resonance down into your bones, into the deep place where memory is not thought but structure. There—threaded through marrow and identity—you sense it: a glowing seam that does not belong to you alone. A lineage. A doorway. A right of passage no one ever consented to carry.

You breathe once, slow and steady, and tighten your grip around it—not with fingers, but with will so absolute it feels like a vow made directly to the land. The Chorus falters. Not in fear. In disbelief. "Little Seer," they sing, voices quivering at the edges— "This is the road that leaves no story behind." You do not answer them.

Answering would be negotiation, and you have chosen refusal.

You ignite the Thread. Not with fire from torch or lightning, but with the heat of renunciation—an inner blaze that consumes meaning, inheritance, and claim. The moment it catches, your entire body arches as if struck. Pain blooms white-hot, not localized, not survivable in any ordinary sense. It tears through you in a single wave, ripping the Thread's shape out of your marrow like a root pulled from earth. The Chorus screams. A soundless, vast rupture tears through their song as names unravel into nothing. The voices do not die as people die. They are erased like marks in sand swept clean by the tide.

The storm recoils. For the first time, it hesitates—not because it fears you, but because it cannot recognize what you have become. Its attention stutters, searching for the familiar resonance that made you legible to it. The resonance is gone. Lightning flickers wildly, no longer measured. Wind slams downward and then scatters as if it cannot decide where to strike. The storm's enormous patience falters, not in rage but in confusion.

You are no longer an axis. You are no longer a door. You are, suddenly, opaque to the sky. The Thread burns to ash inside you. You feel it collapsing inward, disintegrating into a heat that devours not only power but the pathways that once carried it. Something in your mind snaps—not breaking, but severing: the sense of the world as layered with voices, omens, and unseen intent.

Silence falls. Not the oppressive silence of containment. Not the charged silence before a storm. A clean, unfamiliar silence—the kind that exists when nothing hidden remains attentive. The storm shudders one last time, as if reaching for a language it no longer remembers, and then begins to disperse. Clouds unravel into ordinary shapes. Lightning fades into distant, aimless flickers. Thunder rolls away across the horizon, diminishing with each breath, like a great beast losing interest and wandering off. It is not defeated. It is simply... unanchored.

Without blood to speak through, the god-born tempest cannot complete itself. It cannot be born with purpose. It cannot devour the world as prophecy promised, because prophecy has just lost its spine. You drop to your knees on the high rise, gasping. The air tastes plain—no longer sharp with omen, no longer thick with ancestral nearness. Your skin is slick with sweat and rain that has begun to fall softly, undecided, no longer commanded by any will—your heart hammers like a mortal thing startled back into its own body.

You lift your hand. The wind does not adjust. You swallow, searching inward instinctively for Stormsense—your old blessing, your signature thread into the unseen. There is nothing. No flicker behind the eyes. No pressure map in the ribs. No whispered warning from dead mouths beneath rivers. Only you. Only breath. Only the ache of survival.

Far away, Druids feel it, not as pain, but as sudden emptiness. Across Ériu, those trained to read omen and rune pause mid-ritual, hands suspended over offerings that no longer warm or hum. Sacred fires burn the same as any hearthfire. Stones remain stones. Water remains water. Seers wake in the night, not from visions, but from their absence. A woman in the north who once dreamed storms into warning sits up in bed and weeps without knowing why. A young boy who could always hear the faint river-voices stands at the riverbank and hears only water. A druid in a coastal shrine speaks an invocation—and the air does not change. The world has gone quiet. Not dead. Not broken. Just unenchanted.

You descend from the hill slowly. Every step feels heavier than it used to, not because the ground pulls harder, but because you can no longer lighten it with unseen balance. Your senses are sharper in some ways—smoke smells like smoke, not like inherited memory. Rain sounds like rain, not like an omen. But the loss is vast, a missing organ you did not know you had until it was gone.

When you reach the first village below, people are gathered outside, staring at the sky. "The storm stopped," someone says, awed. Others murmur prayers out of habit, then fall silent when no answering chill runs through the air, no sign appears. A few look frightened, as if the absence of divine attention is worse than its wrath. You walk among them unnoticed. That is another new thing: you are no longer marked by pressure. Animals do not flee. Fires do not gutter. People's eyes do not slide toward you as if they sense weather in your bones. You are simply a traveler in a damp cloak—a mortal. You keep walking.

Days pass. Then weeks. News travels in strange, altered ways. Some rejoice. They call it liberation—no more omen-driven fear, no more priestly leverage, no more kings claiming divine right. They tear down a few shrines. They stop paying offerings that once fed hungry authority. They argue openly about law and rule as if their words are finally unshadowed.

Others mourn. They speak of a hollowing-out, as if the world has lost its depth. They continue rituals anyway, out of tradition, out of stubbornness, out of longing. But the rituals become performance rather than communion—symbol rather than channel.

Kings adapt quickly. Without divine approval or land judgment, authority becomes purely human. Some kings soften, realizing they can no longer hide behind sacred inevitability. They negotiate. They compromise. Councils rise where crowns had once been unquestioned. Other rulers harden. They build laws like walls. They enforce obedience through threat rather than omen. In some places, justice improves. In others, oppression sharpens. The difference is no longer checked by gods. It is checked only by people.

You are asked, more than once, if you saw a sign, if you know why the sky quieted. You say little. You do not claim credit. To claim credit would be to create a new kind of priesthood, and you have not burned the Thread to become another source of coercion. You keep moving, learning what it means to live in a world that does not automatically lean toward meaning. At night, you dream—not prophecy, not ancestral memory—only the debris of your own days. Sometimes you wake with a phantom feeling of voices just beyond hearing, and it takes you a long moment to remember they are gone.

Years pass. You age. The work of survival is ordinary now. You mend clothing. You rest sore joints. You laugh at small things and are startled that laughter still comes without magic to sweeten it. You love, perhaps, in a quiet way, without destiny pressing its hand between you and another heart. You return to Tara once, late in life.

The Hill of Tara stands as it always has—wind-brushed, mist-prone, ancient in its stillness. The standing stones remain cracked in places, but they do not glow. They do not shift meaning when you stare too long. The Lia Fáil is a stone among stones, weathered and silent. Ravens perch and watch you without ceremony. You place your palm against the Lia Fáil and feel nothing but cold rock. No hum. No chorus. No demand. For a moment, grief rises sharp as lightning, and you almost wish—almost—that something would answer, even to condemn you. But the stone remains indifferent, and you understand that this is what you chose: a world that does not require divinity to justify itself.

You sit in the grass and look out over Ériu, its villages scattered like embers across the land. People live down there without omens to warn them, without blessings to save them, without prophecy to excuse them. They live anyway. They build laws. They break them. They try again. They blame one another rather than storms wearing faces. They find meaning where they can, and sometimes they do not find it at all. The sky above moves, cloud by cloud, honest in its aimlessness.

You stand and leave Tara at dusk, walking down the hill with the slow certainty of one who has accepted that sacrifice does not always come with glory. The world does not sing your name. The ancestors do not crown you. The storm does not kneel or devour. It simply passes on like weather.

Ériu endures. And so do you, for a time. Then you do what all mortals do. You fade.

Not into legend. Into the ordinary dark— quietly, honestly, and free of the sky's attention at last.

# Chapter 42
## The Bound Horizon

YOU DO NOT REACH upward. That is the first thing the storm notices. Where it expected surrender or resistance, it finds neither. Your breath slows. Your stance widens, not to brace against force, but to release it. You turn your awareness outward—away from marrow and memory, away from the fragile limits of flesh—and into the wide, patient body of the land itself. The storm presses, confused. For the first time since it found you, its pressure meets refusal without hostility. You are not a door closing. You are a door never meant to open.

The plain beneath your feet answers before the sky does. You feel it in the soil first: a deep, resonant tension like a held chord. This place—this high, wind-scoured expanse where stones once tried to speak for the world—has always known storms. It remembers lightning without fear. It remembers pressure without collapse. You sense fault-lines running like scars beneath the earth, ancient boundaries where force gathers and breaks harmlessly against itself. This land has endured not by yielding, but by holding.

You offer the storm not yourself, but a horizon. The redirection is not gentle. Wind snaps outward in a sudden ring, flattening the grass in a perfect circle that widens with every heartbeat. Lightning recoils from your body and lashes instead along invisible lines in the air, tracing arcs that race toward distant ridges and valleys. Thunder rolls low and continuously, no longer gathering above you, but spreading sideways—seeking the edge you have defined. The storm resists, not in anger, but in instinct.

Pressure surges, testing the limits you are shaping, pushing against the invisible wall you are drawing across sky and land alike. Your teeth rattle—blood beads at your nose. The effort is enormous—not because the storm fights you, but because the land must be convinced to accept what you are asking of it. You sink to one knee, palms pressed flat against the ground. You do not command. You negotiate.

You pour understanding into the soil: how the storm gathers, how it fractures, how it burns itself out when denied endless reach. You give the land what the old circles never could—not ritual, not reverence, but comprehension. You show it where pressure may settle, where lightning may spend itself without scarring villages, where thunder may roll without becoming omen or judgment. Slowly—agonizingly—the land answers.

A deep vibration spreads outward, felt more than heard—stones buried beneath the plain hum in resonance, ancient and steady. Hills along the horizon seem to lean inward, their silhouettes sharpening against the metallic sky. The boundary takes shape—not as a wall, but as a limit: a vast, invisible ring where storm-force gathers and disperses, unable to cross beyond what has been set. The storm recoils again, then stills. It does not kneel. It does not bow. It settles.

Clouds lower and stretch, no longer spiraling toward you, but circling the far edge of the horizon you have drawn. Lightning strikes there—again and again—brilliant, deafening, but contained. Rain follows, heavy and relentless, feeding the land rather than drowning it. The air between you and the storm clears, pressure easing until breath returns fully to your lungs.

You collapse forward, hands sinking into wet earth. For a long moment, you are certain you will not rise again. Your body shakes with exhaustion, nerves screaming from the strain of having redirected something meant to wear gods as masks. When you finally push yourself upright, the storm no longer responds to your movement. It no longer listens. That is how you know it has worked. You stand free of the sky's attention—but not of its consequence.

The horizon glows faintly where lightning continues to spend itself, marking a boundary that will never fade entirely from memory. Travelers will see it from miles away: a region where storms linger longer, where thunder rolls more often, where rain falls with uncanny regularity. Some will fear it. Some will worship it. Some will study it. None will cross it lightly.

You leave the plain before dawn. Behind you, the storm remains—vast, restrained, enduring. It will not follow. It will not seek another body. You have denied it the easiest path and given it a harder one: to exist without dominion. The world changes in response.

Villages nearest the bound horizon adapt first. They learn the rhythms of the contained storms, building where rain feeds crops instead of washing them away. Fires are fewer now. Floods predictable. Lightning clears old growth and renews soil rather than burning homes. What once would have been divine terror becomes environmental reality—dangerous, yes, but understandable.

Farther away, storms grow quieter. Not absent. Not powerless. But stripped of their godborn insistence. Weather becomes weather again, no longer burdened with prophecy. The sky ceases to choose favorites. You are spoken of in stories for a time.

Some call you a coward for refusing apotheosis. Others name you savior for sparing the world another storm-god. Most remember you only as the one who taught the sky where to stop. In some regions, children are warned not to wander toward the bound horizon. In others, pilgrims go there seeking clarity, standing at the edge of the storms to remind themselves of scale. You do not correct them.

You live out your days quietly, body scarred but intact. The storm never calls to your blood again. At times, when thunder rolls along the distant boundary, you feel a faint echo in your bones—not longing, not loss, but recognition. Like hearing a voice you once knew well, now speaking to someone else. The land does not crown you. The sky does not remember your name. And yet, balance holds.

There are still disasters. Still suffering. Still, choices that must be faced without guidance or guarantee. But the worst of the godborn threat has been answered—not by conquest or sacrifice, but by containment without ownership. The storm endures, powerful and constrained. The land adapts, scarred but breathing. And humanity continues beneath a sky that has learned, at last, to keep its distance. Not to rule. Not to vanish. Not to burn. But to draw a line across the world and say: Here, and no farther.

# Chapter 43
# The Awakened Land

YOU WAKE TO SILENCE that does not feel empty. The sky above the basin is torn open in irregular patches—clear blue pressing against bruised cloud, light spilling through seams where storm once held dominion. There is no thunder now—no pressure gathering behind the eyes. The godborn tempest is gone, its will broken not by defeat, but by dispersal. Yet the ground beneath you hums.

You push yourself upright slowly, every muscle protesting. Your palms sink into stone that feels warm—not with heat, but with motion, like something breathing just beneath the surface. When you press your ear close, you hear it: a low, layered resonance moving outward in all directions, racing through fault and root and buried riverbed alike. The storm did not die. It spread. You stagger from the basin as dawn creeps in unevenly, light catching on hills that look subtly altered. Grass shivers, though there is no wind. Stones glint faintly, veins of color surfacing where none existed before. A raven watches you from a nearby pillar, head cocked, eyes reflecting more than sky. As you descend, the changes sharpen.

In one valley, rain falls gently on parched fields, coaxing green from soil that had refused seed for years. In another, frost clings too long to the ground, curling leaves black at the edges. Streams swell and recede unpredictably, some running clear and sweet, others choked with strange growths that pulse faintly at night.

You pass a village at the edge of the plain. People stand in doorways, uncertain whether to celebrate or flee. A child laughs as sparks dance across the tips of their fingers—harmless, playful. An elder nearby stares at their hands in terror as old scars seal themselves shut before their eyes. No one knows what to call what is happening. No one knows who to blame. You keep walking.

Word travels faster than you do, not by herald or decree, but by story—fractured, contradictory, alive. In the west, a sacred grove long thought dead erupts with impossible bloom, trees flowering out of season, their bark etched with symbols no druid remembers carving. In the north, a hillside cracks open, releasing lights that drift at dusk like wandering stars, harmless unless touched. Magic has returned. Not as law. Not as lineage. As place.

The old hierarchies collapse quietly. Druids argue among themselves, their rites failing in one region and surging wildly in another. Seers discover their sight sharpened in some lands and dulled in others, as though the world itself is deciding who may listen. Kings issue proclamations that mean nothing beyond their borders, their authority dissolving into local custom and necessity. You realize then the depth of what you have done.

There will be no single Ériu again. The land has become plural. Some communities adapt with startling grace. Councils form, drawing wisdom from those who know the ground beneath their feet best. Traditions are reborn—new songs, new taboos, new celebrations tied to the rhythms of awakened places. People learn to live with power rather than above it, cautious and attentive. Others fail.

Fear breeds cruelty. Magic is hoarded, weaponized, blamed. Charismatic figures rise and fall, claiming mastery over forces that answer only briefly before turning strange and dangerous. Old rivalries sharpen into new wars fueled by uneven blessing and resentment. Through it all, you remain peripheral. You feel no surge of power now, no lingering claim. Whatever thread once bound storm to your blood has loosened, stretched thin across the land. You are not drained—but you are no longer central. The world does not look to you for balance. It balances itself, unevenly, stubbornly, alive.

Druin finds you months later on a road that no longer appears on maps. He has aged. Or perhaps you have not noticed the years passing as they should. He studies you for a long moment before speaking. "You broke the sky," he says. "Yes." You reply. "And the land?" He asks. You kneel, pressing your palm to the earth. It answers—not with words, but with texture, vibration, refusal to be singular. "The land is awake." Druin exhales slowly. "It will never sleep again." "No," you agree. "Nor should it."

He watches the horizon, where lights flicker faintly at dusk. "History will struggle with this," he says. "Scholars will demand causes. Kings will demand borders. They will try to bind what cannot be held." You agree, "They always do."

"And you?" he asks. "What place do you claim in what follows?" You stand, brushing dirt from your hands. "None that lasts." Druin nods—not in approval or condemnation, but in acceptance. He turns away, already composing the first of many accounts that will never quite agree with one another.

Years pass. Generations. Children grow up knowing that some hills sing and others bite. That rivers may heal or poison, depending on how they are approached. That no map is final, no law universal. Travelers trade stories the way they once traded coin, learning where the land is kind and where it demands distance.

The gods do not return. Nor do they vanish. They linger at the edges of things—in storm-glass valleys, in whispering bogs, in places where night falls too quickly or not at all. Not masters. Not servants. Witnesses, perhaps, to a world that no longer asks permission to change.

As for you, your name becomes many names. In some regions, you are remembered as a liberator. In others, a fool. In a few, a warning told to children who wander too far into glowing fields. None of them are entirely wrong.

On a quiet evening, standing at the edge of a forest that hums softly with borrowed sky, you realize the truth you could not see before: You did not save the world. You gave it back its teeth. The land breathes. The sky listens. And history, fractured and alive, moves forward without waiting for permission. This is the age that follows prophecy.

www.ingramcontent.com/pod-product-compliance
Lightning Source LLC
Chambersburg PA
CBHW070655180626
46817CB00006B/2379